bedeviled

THE GOOD, THE BAD, AND THE UGLY DRESS

D0958795

by Shani Petroff
Grosset & Dunlap

An Imprint of Penguin Group (USA) Inc.

GROSSET & DUNLAP

Published by the Penguin Group
Penguin Group (USA) Inc., 375 Hudson Street, New York, New York 10014, USA
Penguin Group (Canada), 90 Eglinton Avenue East, Suite 700, Toronto, Ontario
M4P 2Y3, Canada (a division of Pearson Penguin Canada Inc.)
Penguin Books Ltd., 80 Strand, London WC2R 0RL, England
Penguin Group Ireland, 25 St. Stephen's Green, Dublin 2, Ireland (a division of
Penguin Books Ltd.)
Penguin Group (Australia), 250 Camberwell Road, Camberwell, Victoria 3124,
Australia (a division of Pearson Australia Group Pty. Ltd.)
Penguin Books India Pvt. Ltd., 11 Community Centre, Panchsheel Park, New
Delhi—110 017, India
Penguin Group (NZ), 67 Apollo Drive, Rosedale, North Shore 0632, New Zealand
(a division of Pearson New Zealand Ltd.)
Penguin Books (South Africa) (Pty.) Ltd., 24 Sturdee Avenue, Rosebank,
Johannesburg 2196, South Africa
Penguin Books Ltd., Registered Offices: 80 Strand, London WC2R 0RL, England

Typeset in Concorde.

Cover illustration by J. David McKenney.

Library of Congress Cataloging-in-Publication Data is available.

ISBN 978-0-448-45112-1   10 9 8 7 6 5 4 3 2 1

To Marilyn L. Petroff,
a role model, a support system,
a confidante, a friend,
and most importantly—
the best mother I could ever ask for.
I love you.

A lot of people helped me make this series a reality, and I owe them all a big thanks:

Jodi Reamer, agent extraordinaire, for being there for me.

Judy Goldschmidt for being such an awesome editor. I know my writing has grown because of you.

Francesco Sedita for all of his amazing support and help, along with Bonnie Bader, Allison Verost, Lana Jacobs, Sarah Stern, Meagan Bennett, Alaina Wong, RasShahn Johnson-Baker, and everyone at Penguin who worked on this book. I appreciate everything you've done.

J. David McKenney for another incredible cover illustration.

My talented co-workers for backing me—and in some cases going to bat for me. It means a lot!

Micol, Darci, Anna, Jocelyn, Joanne, and Yvette—who knew taking a class would change my life so much and give me friends for life?

All the wonderful people I've met through this journey—including authors, readers, booksellers, and librarians. You've made it truly memorable.

My friends for their encouragement and support. You're a fabulous bunch.

Jordan, Andrea, and all of my incredible family for believing in me, being a sounding board, and my very own cheering squad. They say you can't pick your family, but if I could—there's no question that I would stick with you guys! You're the best.

And my father who always had a book in his hand and made me fall in love with reading. You will forever live in my heart.

Thank you all!

chapter

1

I unintentionally declared my undying love for him. IN WRITING.

AND. HE. SAW. IT.

I'm talking about Cole Daniels.

My crush. My brand-new boyfriend. My first kiss. Well, sort of. I mean, the kiss happened, and it was one hundred and fifty-eight percent the best thing in the entire world. Only, Cole doesn't remember it, and *not* because it wasn't memorable. At least, I hope that's not why. It's just that I accidentally caused a chain of events that resulted in utter chaos and me going back in time to undo everything—even the greatest kiss ever.

Just one of the nasty hazards of being the devil's daughter and inheriting whacked out powers that I can't control.

That's right. I'm heir to the underworld. I only recently found out—on my thirteenth birthday to be exact. But that isn't important now. What's important now is that COLE THINKS I'M A BOY CRAZY NUTCASE WHO IS COMPLETELY OBSESSED WITH HIM! And I don't blame him.

It started off innocently enough. We were hanging out at his place. He invited me over for pizza and to watch the new Mara's Daughters video. They're our absolute favorite band. We started talking about how Vale, the lead singer, pulled me up onstage when they played here in Goode, Pennsylvania, not too long ago. Lou Cipher, aka Lucifer, aka my dad, set it up. Of course, I didn't share that part with Cole.

"I still can't believe you got to sing with them," Cole had said. I used to be nervous that my connection to the band was the only reason he wanted to hang out with me, but it turned out he actually liked my quirkiness and even seemed to think I was cute. That was a major relief.

"Yeah, it was pretty cool," I agreed. Although, not nearly as cool as sitting on the couch next to him. We were so close, our legs were almost touching. It made it hard to think. I wanted to say something to make him realize how great and irresistible I was, but my mind was stuck on pause. That happens a lot around Cole.

"You even remembered all the words," he said.

"But I probably broke a few eardrums in the process." I wasn't exactly *American Idol* material. Unless you counted the rejects.

Cole laughed. It seemed I made him do that quite a bit. "No, you were really good."

The compliment made me feel shy.

"So . . ." he said, rubbing his hands on his jeans to get rid of all the pizza dust.

"So?" I repeated like a parrot.

Cole didn't answer. Instead he turned his attention to the Phillies game on TV. Not what I had been hoping for. Then without any warning, he just reached over and grabbed my hand. "I'm glad you came over," he said. "I like hanging out with you."

I was in a state of semi-shock, but somehow I managed to nod in agreement. Not that Cole would have noticed. He was still staring at the television. I glanced from him, to our intertwined hands, then back to him.

But as soon as he looked back at me, my eyes instantly shifted downward. I don't know why. I think maybe I was afraid I was going to internally combust from the awesomeness of it all. When I finally got the courage to pick my eyes back up, Cole was still looking at me.

This was it! He was going to kiss me. Finally! (Or . . . Again! Depending on how you look at it.) All the waiting was going to pay off. Except . . .

Suddenly I was overcome with paranoia that I had spinach stuck in my teeth. It's been known to happen—one of the hazards of ordering veggie pizza. I knew I should have gone with my old standby—pineapple.

"I'll be right back," I said to Cole, then rushed to the bathroom. Good thing I did because I may have been Angel Garrett on the outside, but between my two front teeth I was all Popeye the Sailor Man.

I took the matchbook sitting in a tiny little tray on top of the toilet tank (you know what it's there for, I know what it's there for, we all know what it's there for, so I hope it's okay if we leave it at that) and used the corner of it to yank out the offending piece of spinach. Then I took one last glance at myself in the mirror and gave myself clearance to be kissed. "Cue the fireworks," I said to myself. Cliché I know, but also accurate. I really did see imaginary fireworks that first time around.

I slid back onto the couch and picked up Cole's hand (in case he needed to be reminded where we left off). My breath got caught in my chest as his head moved toward mine. This was going to be the most perfect kiss in the history of perfect kisses. Cole Daniels plus Angel Garrett—true love forever!!!

Just as our lips were about to touch, there was a loud, booming explosion, then another one, and another one. They were coming from right outside. I let out a scream and practically threw myself onto Cole's lap. I looked to him for answers, but his eyes were glued to the window.

"What?" I asked and turned to follow his gaze.

"Come on." He ran out the side door and into the backyard with me trailing behind.

Oh my God.

"Where are they coming from?" he asked, his voice almost a whisper. "Do you see these fireworks?"

And he didn't mean some invisible spark between the two of us. He meant real, honest to goodness fireworks. They were going off right over his swimming pool. Only about ten feet above our heads.

This had me written all over it. Literally. Because they weren't ordinary fireworks. They formed a heart shape with **CD + AG. TLF!** inside. And the heart was just frozen in midair.

This could not have been happening. Only it was. Whenever my emotions go into overdrive, my powers go bananas. Not that I can blame myself entirely. How's a girl supposed to stay calm and collected when the cutest boy in the whole eighth grade is about to kiss her?

"Stop the fireworks," I mumbled, hoping my powers would obey. "What?' Cole asked me.

"Nothing," I answered. "Just that it looks like the FIREWORKS ARE OVER." I semi-screamed the last few words. I don't know if that's what did it or not, but my powers kicked back in and the sparkles turned into smoke and faded away.

Cole looked shell-shocked. "They went off out of nowhere," he said, putting his hand through his dark wavy hair.

"That's impossible. It was probably just a neighbor setting them off."

Cole shook his head. "We're the only ones out here. And they went off right in my yard. Plus how do you explain the heart with our—"

"What heart? There was no heart. It was your imagination," I said, trying hard to sound calm. "You didn't see a heart. It was just a random design."

He shook his head. "I know what I saw. You had to have seen it." Man, he could be stubborn.

"You probably just dreamed it all up in your head. Like when people look at the clouds, and see what they want to see," I said. "Maybe you just wanted to see our initials up there."

That got him to shut up.

For one second.

"If it was only my imagination, then how did you know our initials were up there?" Leave it to me to pick someone cute *and* smart.

"Because you told me," I lied. My nerves were making it hard to keep my thoughts straight.

"No, I didn't," he insisted. "I was going to, but you cut me off."

"Cole, this is crazy," I squawked. "You're confused. I'd know if I saw our initials pop up somewhere."

So the wrong thing to say. Because no sooner did the words leave my lips, than did our initials appear again. Just like that. Only this time they were engraved in a tree about four feet from where we were standing. Fortunately, Cole had his back to it. But the sight of my jaw dropping to my ankles caused him to turn, leaving me with no choice but to push him in the pool.

That's right. I pushed him into the pool. With both

hands, I shoved the guy of my dreams, fully clothed, into freezing cold water.

I didn't wait to hear his response. I booked it to the tree. I had to make our initials say something else before he saw it. The question was: How? It wasn't like I carried around a knife, so I clawed at it with my fingernails. It didn't work. Our initials were still there bigger than life.

"What did you do that for?" Cole asked approaching me. He was sopping wet. I felt bad. It was definitely not the right weather for swimming. I hoped he didn't catch a cold. But I couldn't worry about that. There were bigger issues. Like the fact that he was going to see the initials in the tree and know I put them there!

I lunged at the tree, wrapping both arms around it in a big bear hug. My body was the only thing shielding me from ultimate humiliation.

There was no way I was letting him see what was written. It would be horrific.

No. Way worse that that. Horrendously horrific. Horrendously, horrifyingly horrific to the ninety-eighth degree. And then some.

"Well?" Cole asked again.

"I thought I saw someone, and I got spooked. Maybe it was the guy who set off the fireworks."

He didn't seem to be buying it.

"I didn't mean to push you that hard. It was supposed to be a tap to tell you to look and see if you saw him, too, but I guess the tap may have been more of a shove. I'm sorry," I said, adding one more lie to the rest that tumbled out of my mouth at turbo speed.

Cole just stared at me without uttering a word. I needed him to say something.

He finally did. "Why are you wrapped around the tree?"

Not that though. It was better when he was silent.

"Um. I'm still spooked?" I asked more than stated.

He looked around the yard. "There's no one here."

"Okay," I said. But I still couldn't let go. Not without him seeing what was written there and thinking I did it. Then he'd probably figure I was behind the fireworks, too.

"Come on," he said, gesturing for me to follow.

"That's okay," I responded. "I'm fine right here."

He didn't seem to know what to say, but that made two of us. "Why don't we go back inside," he suggested.

I was at a loss. Which was worse? Having Cole think I was some freaky tree-hugger who wouldn't separate herself from the wildlife in his backyard or an obsessed girl who vandalized his property and hired someone to set off fireworks to declare my love for him. It was no contest. I was staying put. "You can go. I'm just going to stay here a little longer."

Cole moved closer to me. "There's no one here. You don't need to be afraid."

If it hadn't been such a traumatic scenario, I would have thought it was sweet that he was trying to comfort me. But at that moment, I just needed him to leave. "I'm not afraid. I just like the tree. You can go." Did those words really come out of my mouth? *I like the tree?!*

"Angel," he said, while trying to pull me from around the trunk, "It's all right. Now just—" His words stopped short. The pulling caused me to shift leaving part of our initials exposed. "What's that?" he asked.

"Nothing," I said.

"What are you covering up?" He sure was stubborn.

I wanted to seep into the floor and disappear never to be seen again. "You know what? You were right,"

I said, trying to lure him away from the tree. "There's nobody or anything around here. Let's go inside." I grabbed onto Cole's hand and tried to pull him away before he got a good look.

But no, all he seemed to care about was inspecting the secret message I encoded on the bark. "Does that say—"

"NO," I screamed. "Totally nothing to see there. How about a soda? I'm really thirsty."

But he ignored me and my lame diversion and moved in to inspect my engraved declaration. "Did you do this?" Cole asked.

"No. Yes. I don't know." How was I supposed to answer that? He knew perfectly well that he didn't do it. So that only left me. But I didn't want to own up to something so embarrassing. We only went out once. Leaving that kind of love message made me look crazy.

Cole stared at me, and I stared at my feet.

"My God," he said. "Did you set up the fireworks, too?"

I didn't want to tell him, but God had nothing to do with it.

"You did, didn't you?" he asked, like he was putting together the pieces of a bizarre, twisted jigsaw puzzle starring yours truly.

I could feel his eyes on me. Only not like before in the I-want-to-kiss-you way. This was more the I-think-you-may-have-escaped-from-the-loony-bin way. He probably thought of me as some obsessive, scary, stalker girl who deserved to be the lead freakazoid in a horror movie.

I didn't know what to do. Cole was waiting for me to answer him. But I couldn't. Instead I ran. And I didn't stop until I got all the way home.

There was no way I could ever talk to Cole again. Not after what just happened. He wouldn't want me as a girlfriend. He wouldn't even want me as a friend. He'd want me to stay as far away from him as possible.

Which was exactly what I was going to do.

chapter

2

Mom sat next to me flipping through *Mysticism Monthly* as I scarfed down a bowl of Lucky Charms before school.

"There was supposed to be an ad for aurasrus.com in here." That's the website she runs that sells good luck charms, potions, crystals, and all that hocus-pocus stuff. I didn't comment. I couldn't. There would be no more talking for me. Ever. I didn't want to accidentally set off any more disasters. Not after what happened at Cole's house. Who knew what other embarrassing situations I'd create for myself?

I was better off silent. Mom didn't even think I was being weird. In fact, she was proud of me. I told her I was doing one of those silent retreats she always goes on and on about. It's a new age thing where people don't speak for a number of days in order to get in touch with themselves. I just let her think my teachers were okay with it.

"This is the second time they left it out," Mom said, still going on about the magazine.

There was a quick burst of smoke and next thing I knew there were three of us at the kitchen table. Lou was now sitting comfortably in our big Buddha chair, making himself quite at home. Stuff like that didn't faze me anymore. I was used to Lou appearing whenever and wherever he wanted. He plucked the magazine right out of Mom's hands. "Let me fix that for you." With a wave of his hand, the back of the magazine now had a full-page ad for aurasrus.com. "Every magazine looks like that now." He gave Mom a wink and a huge grin.

You'd have thought she would have been ecstatic about all the free publicity, but you would have thought wrong. "Undo what you've done this instant," she said, jumping out of her seat and grabbing the set of energy crystals she kept stashed on top of the counter ever since Lou first reappeared in our lives. Mom supposedly filled them with "good" karma. She placed them in a semi-circle in front of Lou. "There will be no powers used in this house. Not ones that come from evil."

She waved her arms around. I think she was trying to stir up the energy from the crystals. With Mom, you could never tell for sure.

"And what about your daughter?" Lou asked. "Does that mean she can't use her powers?"

"Fortunately, for all of us concerned, she takes after me and didn't inherit your evil genes. She's just a normal girl."

I could feel Lou's eyes on me, but I chose to study the marshmallow-y goodness of my cereal instead. See, I never told my mom that I had inherited powers. Even though she said it wasn't a big deal, that it wouldn't make me evil, and that she'd love me no matter what, I knew she didn't really mean it. A woman who spent most of her adult life looking for ways to ward off evil didn't want a daughter who could perform black magic. This conversation confirmed that. I had definitely made the right choice keeping her in the dark.

"Now, will you please leave?" Mom told Lou. "If you want to come over here and see your daughter again, you can use the door and knock like everybod—"

Lou didn't give Mom a chance to finish. In a flash he was gone, and there was a knock at the door.

Mom shook her head and stashed a few crystals in her pocket, as she went to answer it. "I was going to tell you to call first," she said as she swung open the door.

The phone rang.

"Aren't you the comedian!" Mom said.

"Thank you." Lou adjusted his suit jacket. "I do like to entertain those around me. Now that we've gotten those formalities out of the way, may I see my daughter?"

Mom pursed her lips together before speaking. "That's up to her."

I just stormed into the living room to find my backpack. I didn't want to deal with my parents' drama. I had enough of my own.

Not taking my hint, Lou followed me. "That woman is never going to forgive me," he said.

"You got me to come around, maybe she will, too," I said. I figured it was safe to speak to Lou. If anyone was able to counter any catastrophe I sent hurtling their way, it was him.

A few weeks ago, he had come through for me and fixed up my mess. In an attempt to get back at Courtney Lourde, the most evil girl in all of Goode Middle School, I made a whole auditorium full of people disappear and accidentally clued them in about my powers in the process. Lou reversed it all in a matter of seconds. That had to count for something. So after that, I let him convince me to give him a chance at being my dad on a probationary basis. Mom was a different story, though . . .

Before I was born, Lou told her he was done with the devil business. But he lied, and when Mom found out, she took off—with me. So she was less than thrilled when he decided it was time to reappear in our lives.

Since then, Lou promised he wouldn't hurt any good people and that he'd find someone to take over his responsibilities watching over the underworld. But so far I hadn't seen any movement in that direction.

Lou shook his head. "Your mother likes holding a grudge. I don't know if there's any getting through to her."

I paused from my backpack hunt and looked right at him. "If you want to get on her good side, you might want to lay off the magic. We're not fans of powers here," I said, then went back to my search.

I checked under the coffee table, the couch, behind Mom's desk, but I couldn't find my backpack anywhere. I didn't have time to play hide-and-seek anymore, I had to get going. My best friend, Gabi Gottlieb, was waiting for me by the old McBrin house so we could walk to school together. I couldn't be late. There was no way I was facing Goode Middle School alone. Not today. Not after Saturday. "Where's MY BACKPACK?" I shouted.

Then mom's supply closet door swung open and hit me smack in the back of the head. The pain was killer, but there hanging on one of the hooks was my backpack. I didn't think to look there because there's never anything in there but stuff for mom's website. My mom must have put it there in one of her cleaning frenzies, I thought as I tried to rub away the pain. I was definitely going to have a bump. I guess it beat a pair of horns and a tail. But still . . .

"Ouch." Lou gave a low whistle. "Looks like somebody needs to learn how to manage their powers."

"Shhhhhh," I said peering into the kitchen. Fortunately, Mom was sitting cross-legged on the counter chanting her mantra: Goodness and happiness follow me wherever I go. When she was in her "zone," you didn't have to worry about disturbing her. One perk to having a new age Mom. "I don't have powers anymore," I hissed at Lou.

"Then how do you explain the door flying open?" he asked.

"Wind."

"Angel, you're going to have to deal with this. Your powers are not going to go away. Let me teach you how to control them before you hurt yourself." He reached out and touched my head. The pain was instantly gone. "More than you already have."

"How did—" I didn't need to ask. I knew how he did it. Stupid powers. Which I wanted no part of. "I have everything under control. My powers aren't an issue anymore. Really. I've been working on silencing them all weekend. And I have it all figured out."

I wasn't sure who I was trying to convince—him or me.

"Look, why don't we sit down and discuss this with your mother, and then I can begin training you."

"No and no. There's nothing to tell Mom because I've decided to shut off my powers. They're as good as gone."

He put his hands on my shoulders. "Angel, it doesn't work like that."

I pulled away. "It does now." It had to. I couldn't handle powers, I could barely handle a normal day of school without a meltdown over homework, something Cole said, or the nasty comments from the "cool" kids. I didn't want to think about how much damage I could do as the devil's protégé.

25

chapter

3

"Finally," Gabi said when I rode up to the old McBrin house and chucked my bike behind the bushes. "I wasn't sure if you were going to show. Why didn't you call me back? I tried you all weekend. I can't believe you haven't told me about your date with Cole yet. Spill! I want to hear everything."

I didn't answer her. I had to keep my mouth shut so there would be no more fireworks, love graffiti, or head bumps.

"Oh my God—you can't even speak. *That* good?"

I said nothing.

"Okay, now you're being weird," she closely inspected my face for clues. Then did some mental math. "I'm sorry. Do you not want to talk about it? That's okay. We don't have to."

I could tell she didn't mean it at all and just said it

to get me to talk. She gave her little scheme a moment to work and when it didn't, she wigged. "What's going on here? You *never* not want to talk about it. Are you mad at me? Are you giving me the silent treatment?"

I shook my head no.

"Then why won't you say anything?" she pressed on.

I wanted to assure her that I wasn't angry, but I couldn't. My silence was for her own good. Anything I said, even kiddingly, had the potential to backfire. A statement like "I'm afraid I'll accidentally set off a natural disaster," could actually cause a natural disaster.

"Wellllllllllll?" she asked, her hands on her hips. I could tell she was getting annoyed.

I just shook my head.

"Fine, Angel," she said, and began to walk off. "If you don't want to talk to me, then I don't want to talk to you, either. You just wait. When I have big news, you'll be the last to know."

Great, now my powers were getting me in trouble with my best friend. There was absolutely nothing good about being half-devil. I caught up to her, looked her right in the eyes and emphatically shook my head no again. I tried gestures, drawing pictures in the air, and even prayed she'd figure out what I meant.

It still took her a while, but when she threw both hands over her mouth, I knew she figured it out. "Ooooooooh! I get it!" she said, slowly lowering her hands. "It's your powers, isn't it?"

Finally! I put my finger on my nose and started tapping.

"Hmm," she said, "then you're too embarrassed to speak because you . . . you . . ."

I nodded and then signaled an explosion.

". . . cause an explosion when you do?"

Thumbs down.

". . . a disaster?"

Ding. Ding. Ding. I tapped my nose again.

"That's ridiculous. You're being insane. You've had your powers for a while now, and random conversations have not set them off."

Except for Saturday. And that was enough to keep my lips shut.

"Besides," she continued, "can't your thoughts activate them, anyway? And you can't shut those off. You're thinking right now. So you might as well say something."

"It doesn't work like—" My hand shot out over my mouth.

"Ha!" Gabi said sticking her arm out and pointing at me. "You spoke."

Shoot. The non-talking thing was going to be harder than I anticipated.

"And," she went on, "I know you're thinking. You can't stop that."

But Gabi had it wrong. My thoughts weren't my problem. They could only influence my powers once I had already summoned them with something I said. But thoughts alone were harmless.

"You know you want to talk. You know it." Gabi danced around me, repeating herself over and over again.

I did want to speak. I wanted to tell her to be quiet and stop bugging me. But I was afraid I'd permanently silence her or turn her into an ant or something, so I just went to the bushes and checked on my bike instead.

"Just think how hard it will be not to talk to anyone," Gabi said, changing her tactic. "What happens when Mrs. Torin calls on you in class?" Mrs. Torin was our English teacher and also directed the school play. "Are you just going to ignore her?" Gabi paused. I could feel her eyes on me. But I stayed silent.

"What about when she finally sends you to the principal's office. I'm sure your mom won't like hearing that you're misbehaving in school," she continued. "And what if you see someone in danger? Are you going to let them walk in front of a bus because you're afraid to yell, 'Watch out'? Besides, you're never going to be able to keep this silent thing up. I'm going to keep hounding you. It will be super annoying. You'll cave eventually. You might as well spare yourself the drama and talk now."

She had a point. I didn't know how much more of her *convincing* I could take. "Fine," I conceded. "But you don't know what I've been through." As we headed to school, I filled her in on everything from when my nerves got all jittery when Cole was about to kiss me, to the horrible tree incident, to getting whacked in the head with the closet door this morning.

"Wow, that stinks," Gabi said.

"Tell me about it. I'm not going to even be able to look at Cole anymore without reliving that moment."

"Why don't you just take Lou up on his offer to teach you how to control your powers?"

That wasn't an option. "I can't. He's already too involved in my life. Besides, he *is* the devil. I know he seems to be all good and semi-reformed now, but I can't take any chances. What if he's secretly plotting to turn me evil? It's too risky. I'm just going to have to get by without speaking."

"But that's impossible."

I stopped walking and stared at the ground. "Then what am I supposed to do?" I hissed. "Never show myself in public again? Run off to the woods and make friends with the squirrels?"

No sooner had I said that than two squirrels scampered up to me and rubbed against my ankles. I jumped away so quickly you'd have thought there were hot coals under my feet. Yuck. Gross. Eww. Snow White, I was not. When I looked over at Gabi, she was laughing hysterically. "This is not funny."

"You're right," she said, erupting in another fit of laughter. "But at least we know for sure what sets off your powers."

"What are you talking about?" I was now jogging in place. I hoped the movement would scare away any other rodent-type creatures that decided to come my way.

"You already know your powers tend to go berserk when your emotions are in overdrive. You were annoyed when you summoned the squirrels,

31

angry when the closet hit you, and superexcited and nervous about kissing Cole when the fireworks went off. So, you don't have to stop thinking or talking, you just have to stop getting worked up. But that'll probably be hard, since you're the most emotional personal I ever met in my life."

"Am not!" I protested, crossing my arms in front of me. Okay, maybe she had a teeny, tiny point. I have, on occasion, been known to overreact. And some of what she said made sense.

As we continued to school, I kept thinking about it. Gabi was right. The answer to my problem was simple. I could control my powers. I just had to stay calm and not let my emotions get the best of me.

Although, that looked like it was going to prove easier said than done. Because, standing right on the steps to school was Courtney and her band of followers looking ready for a fight.

chapter

4

"This school really should have a back entrance for the ugly people," Courtney said as I hiked up the steps. "Between that," she pointed at me, "and the ginormous wart that follows her wherever she goes," she gestured toward Gabi, "this school is going to get a bad reputation."

"Seriously." Lana Perkins, Courtney's pseudo-bodyguard, nodded in agreement.

"Aww, look," Jaydin Salloway joined in. She was Courtney's BFF and one of those girls who made guys stop and stare when she walked by. Even I had to admit Jaydin was super-pretty. But she was also super mean. "I think we're making her mad," she said with a smirk so condescending, I wanted to—

No, I had to stay calm. I took a deep breath. I couldn't think about how I wanted to make her nose hair grow all the way down to her kneecaps. I needed to play nice. This was the perfect test to keep my powers in check. If I could handle Courtney and company, I could handle anything.

"It's a good thing I'm not as hideous as Angel or as nerdy as Gabi," Courtney blabbed on as she moved over to stand in my way. "Otherwise, D.L. never would have noticed me. Then we never would have gone out and he never would have kissed me yesterday. He wouldn't want to put his lips near a freak show, no one would."

"Please," I spat back at her. "How pathetic. Is that your way of telling me D.L. finally got sick of all your stalking and gave you a mercy kiss? Like I care if you kiss some troll." Okay, I know I should have ignored her all together, but I couldn't help it. Someone had to stand up to Courtney. Besides, I kept my emotions in check through it all so it was good practice.

"D.L. is not a troll."

"Right," I said, trying to be as sarcastic as I could. D.L. Helper was some guy Courtney met at camp. When we were friends for a whole millisecond not too long ago, she told me they went out over the summer, but he stopped paying attention to her once school started. I saw his Facebook picture. He wasn't that special. Unless you went for the floppy blond hair, big blue eyes, tanned look. Okay, fine. He was cute. But Courtney didn't need to know I thought so.

"Just because Cole has made you his charity case and is being nice to you, does not mean you are special," Courtney said, her voice steady and dripping with venom. "You are still a pathetic wannabe, and no one is ever going to truly want to be around you. Not me, not Cole, not anyone. Got that, loser?"

I could feel the blood rising inside of me. "I'm so sick of you. I wish someone wou—"

"Let's go," Gabi said, dragging me with all her might into the building. "We're going to be late." When we were a safe distance away from Courtney, Gabi reprimanded me. "What were you thinking? Do you know what could have happened? I thought you were going to stay calm!"

"I *was* calm." I picked up the pace as we walked to homeroom.

"Your face was redder than a cherry tomato."

"It was hot outside."

"Angel," she chided me. "You can't let Courtney get to you. You're way too sensitive. Who cares what she says?"

I stopped outside of the classroom. "Fine. So I got a little worked up. It won't happen again. I'll just stay away from her and anyone else who might make my powers flip out."

And that definitely included Cole.

chapter

5

The day was shaping up to be one of my all-time top ten worst ones ever. First, dealing with Courtney at the steps, then trying to ignore Cole in homeroom.

"Hey," he said when I took my seat behind him.

I gave him a slight nod. I had to keep my cool, which would have been a lot easier if my heart wasn't thumping like I just ran a marathon. He was going to want answers about what happened the other day. But I couldn't give them for two reasons. One: There wasn't a good explanation. And two: I didn't trust myself to speak around him. That would just be asking for my powers to act up again.

"What was that all about the other day?" he asked, rolling his pen between his fingers.

I didn't even know exactly what he meant. The fireworks? The tree? The running off? There was a lot of messed up stuff to choose from. Part of me was glad I couldn't talk to him. Saturday's events had run over and over again in my head nonstop all weekend. And you know how people say everything gets better with time? Well, they're wrong. The playback only got more and more cringeworthy each time I ran it through my head. Having to be so close to Cole made it even worse.

I pretended not to hear him. But he kept pressing me.

"When did you engrave the tree? It wasn't there on Friday. Did you sneak over in the middle of the night and do it?"

I ignored him and reached down into my backpack. I tried to make it look like I was busy searching for something important. I hoped Cole would see that and drop the subject, but he just kept hounding me with his questions.

"I can't figure out how you got the fireworks to go off. Did you have some kind of detonat—"

That's all I heard. Before he could even finish his sentence I got up, grabbed the bathroom pass, and left. I had no other choice. Being in the same room as Cole made it hard to breathe.

I wanted to tell him the truth. That I wasn't crazy— there was a good reason for my bizarre behavior. But I couldn't. And until I could guarantee that I wouldn't set off my powers simply by talking to him, I had to stay away.

For some reason, though, he seemed really determined to talk to me. Maybe his mom wanted me to pay for ruining their tree. He finally managed to catch up to me in the hall before last period. Cole looked at me, then Gabi. It was pretty clear he didn't want to have the conversation in front of her, so she took the hint and backed up a bunch of steps. I knew she was totally still listening, though.

"What's going on?" he asked me.

I just stared at him. I put one hand on my hip and the other by my side in an attempt to look all breezy, but I'm pretty sure it came across as panicked.

"You've ignored me all day."

The hand by my side instantly made its way to my mouth, and I started grinding on two of my fingernails. I was afraid to speak. My nerves were flying way beyond the speed limit. One wrong word and who knew what kind of problems I could cause Cole. I was ignoring him for his own safety. Why couldn't he see that?

We stood there for a moment not saying anything. Then Cole mumbled, "Whatever" and walked away.

"Wait," I yelled, unable to stop myself. I couldn't let him leave. Not like that.

He turned back to me. "What?"

The hallway was about to get busy. I could see Max Richardson heading my way. Unfortunately, Max had a major crush on me. He was nice and all, but let's put it this way, if the school held an election for biggest nerd, Max would win—no contest. I didn't need him butting into my conversation with Cole. And he wasn't the only one approaching. I could see Cole's best friend, Reid Winters, and Lana coming, too.

"I, it's just . . ." I didn't know what to say. The wrong words would only make things worse.

"Hey, Angel," Max interrupted, oblivious to the social taboo of interrupting a conversation between a girl and her crush, especially, but not limited to, when the girl was trying very hard to correct the impression she gave of being a complete psycho. "Got a whole bunch of new CDs. Want to take a lo—"

"Not now, Max," I snapped. I didn't mean to. I've always been nothing but nice to Max. I guess I couldn't help it, though. I was like one giant raw nerve.

"Nice," Cole said, the sarcasm fully on. "Really nice." He ran his hand through his hair. "You know what? You're just not the person I thought you were at all."

NO! Now he thought I was a terrible person. "I'm sorry," I spit out. "I didn't—"

"Look what we have here," a voice I knew all too well called out from behind me. "A lover's spat?" It was Courtney, and Jaydin was right next to her.

"Ooh," Jaydin said cocking her head to one side and giving Cole a smile that made me want to beam her to another continent.

"Stay out of it," I warned them.

"What fun would that be? Finally coming to your senses, Cole?" Courtney asked, moving in closer to him.

"Not now, Courtney," he said, staring up at the ceiling.

Courtney looked around the hallway and her eye's narrowed in on Max, which wasn't exactly hard. He was the tallest guy in the whole school. "I get it," she said. "Angel finally realized who her true soul mate is."

Lana, who had been watching everything, chimed in. "Of course, she's perfect for the Jolly Green Giant. It's a match made in loserville."

"Only, he might be too good for her," Courtney piped back in. "She is exceptionally spazzy, not to mention out of her mind, thinking she's way better than she is."

"Quit it," I yelled. Why wasn't Cole the one jumping to my defense? Did he believe what she was saying? Courtney's taunts felt like they were hammering into my temples. I couldn't take it anymore. "You think you know me? You don't know *anything*. None of you." I fought the tears from escaping my eyelids. "I'm sorry, Cole. I gotta go. Come on, Gabi."

But Gabi didn't even acknowledge me.

"Gabi!" I said again. She just gazed around with a clueless expression on her face. I scanned the rest of the group. They all had that same completely clueless expression, too.

No. No. NO.

What had I done?

chapter
✦6✦

I shook Gabi by her shoulders. "Say something."

"Angel?" she responded as the bell went off.

Yes. That was good. My spell, curse, whatever it was, was only temporary. "Thank God, you remember. Let's go."

"Aren't you Angel? Daughter of the devil?"

Uhh?! Why was she asking me that out loud? Why was she asking me at all?

Before I could respond, the rest of the group stirred back to life. Somewhat. "I think I know Angel," Reid said, his voice flat and monotone.

"Pretty," Max said, running his fingers through my hair.

"I think Angel is a wannabe who wishes she were me," Courtney interjected. Only her voice didn't have the same bite it usually had when she was insulting me. Instead, it was almost lifeless.

I had no idea what was going on. Then it hit me. My powers took my words way too literally again. I had said, "You think you know me. You don't know anything." So now they actually *thought they knew me*, but apparently *not anything else*!

This was bad. Way bad.

I took another look at my classmates. They just stood there, their bodies limp and their eyes vacant, staring into space. If all that was left in their brains was information about me, they were basically helpless. Would they even know how to eat? Pick out clothes to wear? Flush the toilet? I was in way over my head.

"Why aren't you all in class?" the principal, Mr. Stanton, asked as he headed in our direction.

My seven groupies, Gabi, Cole, Courtney, Lana, Reid, Jaydin, and Max, just stared at me.

"Um, yeah, it was my fault," I explained. "I had to tell them something, but we're good now. On our way to class as we speak." I tried to usher the herd of zombies to English.

But it wasn't an easy task. Gabi kept walking into the wall. Courtney started spinning, and Lana and Jaydin followed suit. Apparently, some things never changed. Max plopped himself on the ground, Reid tripped over him, and Cole just rested against a doorway.

"What's going on here?" Mr. Stanton demanded. "Are you all looking for a detention?"

"No, sir," I answered, trying to lift Max off the ground to no avail. He was heavy. I racked my brain for something to say before Stanton interrogated my unresponsive classmates. Or worse, before Gabi opened her big mouth again and filled the principal in on my family secret. "This is part of our English project. It's a play I wrote. It's experimental." I started to applaud. "Good job everyone. Do it just like that in class. Great rehearsal."

I don't know if Stanton bought my story or not, but I fled the scene before I could find out. "Follow Angel, everyone," I chirped, feeling like a bizarro pied piper. "Come this way. Come with Angel. You know Angel, right? Angel is me. Follow me." I just had to get them through last period. Then I'd have time to figure out how to fix everything.

The group went with me to English, but when we got inside they just stood there.

"Well, take your seats," Mrs. Torin told us. "We don't have all day."

I led each zombie to their desk as the whole class watched. They must have thought we had lost our minds. Which was true in a way. I tried to laugh it off. "We're doing an experiment for science class. It's about survival of the fittest and how some people become leaders and others become followers and it's my turn to lead and guide."

"Do it on your own time," Mrs. Torin interrupted.

"Yes, ma'am," I answered, as I put Gabi, the last of the herd, in her seat.

Mrs. Torin started her lesson on *Romeo and Juliet*. She called on Jaydin first. "What form does the prologue take?" she asked. Jaydin just stared into space. "Well?" Mrs. Torin pressed on.

"It's a sonnet," I yelled out.

"Good, and what else can you tell me about it? Reid?"

No answer.

"Cole." Silence. "Courtney."

She was picking on everyone under my evil influence. Not that I was surprised. Mrs. Torin loved calling on people who didn't look like they were paying attention.

"Uh. I know," I said out loud. "Shakespeare used rhyming couplets." I was totally on a roll.

"Right," Mrs. Torin said. "What else? Someone other than Angel. Gabi, what about you?"

Gabi didn't answer, either. She couldn't.

Mrs. Torin slammed her copy of the play shut. "Did any of you do the reading assignment?" A few kids raised their hands. Mrs. Torin, looking frustrated, called on them instead.

At the end of class, Mrs. Torin gave the class a hard stare. "I want you all to read the next two scenes. And for those of you who didn't do your homework over the weekend, I suggest you catch up pronto. There will be a quiz tomorrow."

She walked out with the rest of the students—the normal ones—when the bell rang. I was stuck with the nitwits.

"Return to normal," I commanded over and over again, but it wasn't working. They still looked at me with glassy eyes. "Come on," I shouted.

Still nothing. What if they were like this forever? I had to fix them. This was way worse than what happened with Cole on Saturday. This . . . this could virtually ruin seven people's lives. Eight if you counted mine. Because there was no way I'd be able to live with myself knowing I was responsible for turning my classmates into puppets. I definitely deserved to be sent to prison for this. Only Gabi and the rest of them would probably follow me and just stare and point and make me feel even guiltier than I already did. I was panicked. And left with no other choice.

I knew what I had to do.

Filling my lungs with a deep breath, I shouted, "Lou! Help me!"

chapter
7

"You've got to fix this, you have to make them normal," I begged when Lou popped in the room. "I really messed up. I've emptied their brains."

"Completely?"

"Well, they seem to know who I am. But that's it."

He let out a low whistle as his eyes scanned over my classmates who were sitting there like stuffed animals. "Impressive. Total erasure of memories is very advanced. Very dangerous, too."

My nails were now nonexistent. Had I made Max, Gabi, Cole, and everyone else brain-dead for the rest of their lives?

After my powers went haywire a while back during the school musical, I had asked Lou to erase what happened from everyone's minds. He wouldn't do it—said that it could have serious consequences.

And that was just a matter of blocking out a few minutes from people's memories. I just erased every bit of information ever to have crossed my classmates' minds. What if it wasn't reversible?

"You can undo this, right?" I looked up at him, my eyes pleading my case. If Lou couldn't help me, I was done for. How could I go on, knowing I destroyed seven lives? The answer was simple. I couldn't. If Lou didn't fix this, my life was over, too. "Please."

"Well, since you asked so nicely . . ."

A squeal escaped from my mouth. "Thank you, thank you so much."

"Hold on there a second." Lou held up a finger and wagged it. "There is one condition."

I should have known there'd be a catch. The devil didn't do anything without getting something in return. But whatever it was, I couldn't say no. Not with so many lives on the line. I crossed my arms and waited for Lou to seal my fate.

"From now on, you'll let me train you on how to use your powers."

I was hardly in the position to argue that I had my powers under control. Trying to stay calm wasn't making my "special gift" go away, no matter how much I wanted that to be the case. It was time to give in and trust Lou—at least somewhat. "You win. I'll train with you."

"Lovely," he said. "Now let's take care of your little problem. Take my hands."

I did as he instructed.

"Now I'm going to transfer all of my evil into you—"

"What!?" I shouted, pulling my hands out of his and backing away. I didn't want to turn into a she-devil. Well, more of one than I already was.

Lou let out a hearty laugh. "I'm just playing. Come back."

Funny. Real Funny.

I cautiously stepped back toward Lou and put out my hands.

"Relax," he told me. That would have been a lot easier if he hadn't made the crack he just made. "Now, I need you to clear your mind. Close your eyes, take a few deep breaths." He paused while I did as instructed. "Now, I'm going to let my powers combine with yours to restore the knowledge that's been taken away from your friends." Moments later I felt a surge run through me to Lou and back again.

"Okay, freak show. What's your problem now?"

That voice could only belong to one person.

I opened my eyes. Courtney was back to her old tricks, but Lou was gone. Everyone else appeared to be back to normal as well, and they were all staring at me standing in the middle of the room, looking like a moron with my arms outstretched before me.

"I'm talking to you," Courtney spat. "What's. Your. Problem?"

"Nothing," I answered. "Just going home." It didn't matter that she was being obnoxious again. I was just glad to have her back. I almost gave her a hug. Almost.

"*You're* skipping class?" Jaydin asked.

"Class is over," I told her.

Courtney rolled her eyes at me. "No it's not. You are sooo weird."

Reid and Lana whispered to each other. Apparently, neither of them remembered getting to English class. Or anything that happened afterward. Which I guess was a good thing. Only, how was I going to explain it?

"Where's the rest of the class?" Cole asked, looking around at everyone. Everyone but me. He obviously still remembered our fight. My momentary relief over not ruining my classmates' lives was overshadowed by the realization that Cole now viewed me as an awful human being. *Which was worse than having him think of me as a lovesick Chihuahua that wanted to be at his side all the time.*

"Yeah," Max echoed. "What's going on? Weren't we just in the hallway? How'd we get here?"

I had to tell them something. So, even though I was in no mood, I put on a smile and tried to chuckle. "You guys are funny. Quit pretending you don't remember sitting through Mrs. Torin's lecture on Shakespeare."

Gabi scrunched up her nose at me.

"Go with it," I mouthed to her.

"Yeah," Gabi said. "Mrs. Torin went on and on. I guess it was easy to block out. Umm. We need to go. See you all tomorrow."

Thank God for best friends. "Bye, everyone," I said, grabbing Gabi's arm. I gave Cole a small wave, but this time it was him doing the ignoring. "Oh, and don't forget there's a quiz on the next two scenes of *Romeo and Juliet* tomorrow," I managed to get out.

I'm glad I remembered that one. I didn't need to be responsible for them all failing English. It would just be one more reason for Cole to hate me. Even if he didn't know it.

chapter

"What's eight times seven?" I asked Gabi as we headed back to the old McBrin house.

"Enough," Gabi yelled. I had been quizzing her the whole way to make sure there wasn't any permanent damage from my brain erasure. "I told you I remember everything that happened before you blitzed my brain."

"How do you know? If you don't remember something, you're not going to remember that you used to remember it."

"Huh? You're not making any sense," Gabi said, tugging at her braid.

"Or maybe I am, and you just can't tell."

"Rori, stop!"

Whoa. "What did you just call me?"

"Rori."

My stomach did a one-hundred-and-eighty degree turn. "You know who I am, right?"

"Yeah, my annoying little sister."

"Cut it out." I smacked her arm. She was totally messing with me. "You scared me."

"Sorry," she said, giggling. "You're just stressing way too much—like usual. It wasn't a big deal. You were able to fix everything."

"You mean Lou was."

"Same difference," she said, stopping at the old McBrin house. "Everything's back to normal."

Only normal for me meant being the devil's kid. Cole would never understand that.

"And I still think you can make things better with Cole," Gabi said, reading my mind. We were in sync like that a lot.

"No, I can't," I explained. "With you, it's different. You already know about my powers, so if they go nuts, I don't need to cover up. But with Cole, I have to keep feeding him these corny excuses. He already thinks I'm an evil freakazoid because of it. But that's better than letting him catch on to my secret. At least I think it is."

I took a deep breath to suck back the tears.

"Gab, I just have to face facts. Until I can control my powers, I'm going to have to leave things the way they are and keep avoiding Cole at all costs.

55

chapter

9

When I got home, Lou was waiting for me in my room. "Time for lesson one," he said, whipping a Harry Potter robe out of thin air and wrapping it around himself.

I grabbed a notebook and pencil from the clutter on my floor and hopped on my bed. Then I just looked at Lou and waited. It was hard not to stare at him. He was my *father*. The man I had wondered about for thirteen years. And now there he was, right in front of me. If it wasn't for the whole devil thing, I would have been pretty excited. But while he said he was past all that evil stuff, it was still hard to trust him.

"What's on your mind?" he asked.

"Nothing," I said quickly.

"It's something," he said.

"I was just wondering," I looked down at my empty notebook, "if you quit the devil business yet."

He smiled. "I told you," he said. "Not to worry. I no longer take good souls. I just watch over the bad ones. Someone needs to. Otherwise they'd cause all kinds of havoc here on Earth. It's noble work. You should be proud of your old man."

It was kind of hard to be proud of a guy known for his wicked ways. But Lou said he changed. And I wanted to believe him. It was just, well, if anyone would be able to lie and get away with it, it would be him. "But weren't you going to get someone to take over for you all together?"

"Absolutely," he said. "Just as soon as the right person comes around, I'm out."

That sounded more like a stalling tactic than a promise.

"Hey," he said, lifting my chin up. "You don't need to worry about me, I promise. But you do need to worry about your powers. You need to work on controlling them. And that means starting with the basics. Got it?"

I nodded my head.

"Good. You're going to have to do everything I say. That includes committing to your lessons and practicing at least two hours a day—preferably more."

Just what I was looking for—more homework! Whatever. I knew it was a necessary evil if I ever wanted to talk to Cole again.

"Your biggest problem is that you lack focus and commitment. You really have to concentrate and want your powers to work in order for them to function properly," Lou explained. He pulled out his hPhone, which was like an iPhone only with supernatural applications. "Step one," he read off of the screen. "Moving a pencil across the room."

Seriously? "You're joking, right?"

"Not at all. That's what you'll be working on until you master it."

I had hoped lesson one would be something useful like cleaning your room with the snap of a finger or turning paper into dollar bills, not something tediously boring. But I gave it a try, anyway. I placed the standard number two on my open palm, focused all my attention on it, and thought "move." It didn't budge. Twenty-three more tries all had the same result.

"You're not concentrating," Lou said.

"Am too," I protested.

"Try gesturing with your other hand, it will get you focused."

"Fine." I made a big sweeping motion in the direction I wanted the pencil to go. The only thing that moved was my arm.

58

"Maybe I need to say something," I grumbled. "That seems to set off my powers."

"And look how well that's been working," Lou said. "This is about using your mind and your emotions to control your powers. To really get you centered on what you want to happen. It's about concentration. Not words."

"Wait a minute," I protested. "I'm not doing this if it means my thoughts will start setting off my powers. I have enough issues."

"Practice and that won't be a problem."

I was skeptical, but I kept working at it. So much so that my arm was getting tired.

"You need to really want this. Visualize the pencil moving. You're not feeling it. You need to work harder."

He was totally getting on my nerves.

"Focus, Angel," he snapped.

"I am," I said.

"Not enough, you're not."

He needed to get off my back—he was driving me insane.

"Angel—"

"What?!!!" I yelled out, my arm in mid-sweeping motion. "Leave me alone." Then I picked up my notebook and sent it flying at my door—no powers needed.

"Everything okay?" my mother called out. "What's going on?"

"Nothing," I shouted back down to her. "I'm fine. Just getting something from my closet." She couldn't know what I was up to. That would open up a huge can of worms.

"Congratulations, you did it!" Lou said.

"What are you talking about?" I asked. "I threw the notebook with my arm, not my powers."

"I'm not talking about the notebook. I'm talking about the pencil. Take a look." Lou pointed at my hand. The pencil was hovering an inch above it.

"I did that?" As I looked at it, it fell to the ground.

"Yep," he said. "When you were angry and frustrated, it set the pencil in motion. Use those feelings. Remember how you felt, the sensation that went through you. You'll get the hang of it in time. Pretty soon you'll be able to send the pencil flying across the room, and it won't even matter what emotions you're feeling. You'll be able move it with thought alone, but that's down the line. For now your emotions will help you activate your powers."

I nodded. I needed to get this down, so I could move onto bigger lessons and ultimately learn how to keep my powers dormant. Then I could be normal again.

"Now don't worry about setting off your powers in school. I'll keep my eye on you to make sure you don't cause any more problems."

"No," I protested. There was no way I wanted Lou watching my every move. "You are not to watch me."

"But what if something goes wrong? Don't you want me there?"

That was a no-brainer. "No! Promise me you won't spy on me."

"Okay. I won't. I promise." He picked the pencil up off the ground and handed it back to me. "Now keep practicing."

I did as I was told even though anything, even my math homework, seemed more entertaining. But since this was my key to getting back to Cole, it was now the most important assignment of my life.

chapter

10

I didn't have to worry about ignoring Cole in homeroom the next day. He didn't even look at me. As I walked over to my seat, his eyes never lifted from the doodle he was drawing.

It made me sad. Sure, I knew I had to stay away from him. And I was still beyond mortified about the whole initials thing, but I hoped he knew there was more to the story. That he wouldn't care that I acted crazy or ignored him or snapped at Max. I wanted him to *make* me tell him what was really going on. But that wasn't going to happen. I had pushed him away.

As I sat there studying the back of his head, it didn't seem to matter that I had majorly embarrassed myself in front of him. What mattered was that I couldn't make it right. I had no way of letting him see that I was still the same girl he liked last week. Not with my powers all over the place the way they were.

When the bell rang, I ran out of the room as fast as I could. It was too painful to be around Cole knowing he was done with me. I needed to get away so badly, I didn't even look where I was going. I just barreled down the hall—smack into Courtney. And I don't mean figuratively. A real full body slam. Her purse and my books went flying everywhere.

"Watch where you're going, cretin," she spat.

"I'm sorry," I said, handing her bag back to her.

"You will be."

"I said I was sorry," I muttered, as I grabbed my stuff that now littered the ground.

She hovered over me, and kicked my copy of *Romeo and Juliet* right as I went for it. "Oops."

"Knock it off."

"What are you talking about?" she asked, pretending to be all innocent as she kicked it again, this time sending it halfway down the hallway.

I stood up to face her. By this point we were attracting a crowd. "Go get it," I said.

She laughed right in my face. "Like that's gonna happen. Get a clue, Angel. You're such a loser. No one listens to a word you say. And any second now, Cole is going to come to his senses and dump you.

Honestly, I don't even know how he can stand being around you."

Apparently Cole hadn't spread the word about what happened between us. At least not yet. Thinking about Courtney finding out made me feel even lower. "Well, what about poor D.L.?" I spat. "Having to put up with you? He must be a saint."

I should have learned my lesson yesterday that messing with Courtney brings nothing but trouble. But I couldn't help it. There was a whole group of people watching, and after the week I was having, I couldn't let Courtney push me around without standing up for myself.

"Uck." She covered her ears. "You're making my ears hurt with your pathetic comebacks." She reached into her pocket and threw a penny at me. "Here, use that to go buy a life."

A few people laughed. "Please," I countered, my anger rising. "Is that what you used to bribe D.L. to be your pretend boyfriend?"

"Whatevs," she said.

I knew better than to sink to her level, but I couldn't stop myself. I mean my life was falling apart. I couldn't take her messing with me, too. It was bad enough, I was a loser. I didn't want to be a loser who didn't defend herself. I needed to hold on to some self-respect. "I bet D.L. isn't even real," I said, staring Courtney down. "You probably made his Facebook page yourself using a picture of some random guy."

"Oh, okay," she said, humoring me. "But newsflash, Angel, you're the only one here who needs to create imaginary friends. If you haven't noticed, people actually like *me*. D.L. included."

"Yeah, then let's see him. Bring him here. Prove you didn't make him up."

She shook her head. "I don't need to prove anything to a freak show like you."

With that, she turned on her heels and walked away.

chapter

11

"Guess who I spoke to in Hebrew School," Gabi said. I'd been trying to get that darn pencil to move for an hour and a half without luck so I was grateful for Gabi's call.

"Who?" I asked. But I had a feeling I already knew.

"Cole."

My hand squeezed around my phone so tightly, I thought I might break it. "What did he say?" Part of me didn't want to know, but the other part knew I'd never get to sleep that night if I didn't find out.

"He asked about you."

"He did?" I have to admit, I'd been pretty jealous that Gabi got to go to Hebrew School. Even though she did nothing but complain about it. I mean, not only did she get to spend extra time with Cole, but she got to have a major party at the end. It sounded pretty cool to me, no matter what she said. "He hates me, doesn't he?"

"Well," Gabi hemmed and hawed. "He did want to know why you were acting so weird."

Just great. I flung myself back on my pillow. "What did you tell him?"

"That you had some stuff going on."

"And . . ." I prodded. "How did he respond to that?"

"He just walked away."

After a quick pause, Gabi started talking again. "But it's not all bad. If he's asking about you, that must mean he still likes you. Even after everything."

Or, it was more likely, that he wanted me to find out from Gabi that he thought I was messed up. I was so upset, I had to hang up. This was a disaster. How was I ever going to make things better with Cole? I needed a plan of action. A list of ideas that could make everything right. I grabbed my notebook. Where was that stupid pencil? I checked under the bed, but it wasn't there. Then I looked up, and did a double take.

There it was, hovering over my head.

It was just like before when I was angry about Lou

nagging me. Only this time Cole was the motivation. It sent the pencil right in the air. *If just thinking about him meant I could make my powers work, I was definitely on the right track.* Finally, something was going right. My luck was turning. Soon I would have total control of my powers, and then there would be nothing keeping me from getting Cole back.

My focus shifted to the pencil flying above me. *Move across the room,* I thought. Instead, it dropped to the ground. Okay. Not quite what I wanted, but it still moved.

With all the concentration I could muster, I thought *rise, pencil, rise.* The stupid thing wouldn't budge. Not even an eighth of a millimeter. Not even when I thought about Cole being mad at me. But I kept at it. Practice makes perfect, after all. Only, after five more tries, it was still planted on my floor.

Then it hit me. Maybe I was bored. Maybe if I tried to do something more interesting, it'd be easier to concentrate. Never mind what Lou said, I had to do what was right for me. I needed to try something fun.

I did a survey of my room. Lying in a heap in the corner was a Mara's Daughters T-shirt I had worn so many times, I had gotten a hole in it.

I grabbed it and spread it out on my bed. That

was it. I was going to make it brand-new. Better than brand-new. I was going to make it the coolest shirt ever, like the one Vale wore in the band's video.

Morph. Morph. Morph. Hmmm. Okay, so it wasn't working. That was fine. I'd get it. I closed my eyes and visualized the shirt I wanted. Black, one-shoulder, with a rhinestone *M* emblazoned on the front. I could see it. I could almost feel it. I opened my eyes, but I was still looking at a ruined faded T-shirt.

Please work, I begged my powers. *Morph!* Slowly the black restored to its original crispness. It was working. Sort of. My T-shirt was now black again, but that was it. It still had a hole. And it was still just a T-shirt. I wanted something hot. Something rocker chick. Not rocker chick fan.

I needed to do something more, so I made up an incantation on the spot. I had no clue if it would help, but I figured it couldn't hurt. People with powers on TV were always using them.

"Take this T-shirt and make it change,
turn it into something . . .

The rhyming thing was harder than I thought. I had to be careful. I didn't want to create something strange.

"Um, take this T-shirt and make it new,

69

Yes, that's what I want to do."

That was better. I was getting the hang of it . . .

"Make it cool, a really hip brand,

Like what Vale wore in the Mara's Daughters band."

This was actually kind of fun.

"I need to learn this to be with Cole,"

Hmm. Cole. Mole. Hole. Wait. I got it!

"Because I'd do anything for him—well, short of trading my soul."

So come on sweater do it for me,

Change into what I want you to be."

I chanted it out loud once, pretty impressed that I was able to come up with a rhyme so quickly. I tried to do it again, but I forgot some of the words. I really should have written it down. The waiting was the worst part. Was it going to change? I watched patiently, but again, nothing happened.

Then I remembered what Lou had said about moving the pencil. He told me to gesture with my hand to help me focus. Would that work for the T-shirt? I decided to try. I waved both hands over the shirt, pretending I was molding a piece of clay. I pushed my hands closer together to symbolize shrinking it (I wanted it form-fitting), made my

70

fingers into imaginary scissors to remove the sleeves and get rid of one of the shoulders all together, made an *M* in the center where I wanted the rhinestones, and believe it or not, it started to work!

The hole in the material started to grow—making one of the shoulders disappear. The sleeves started unraveling, the edges of the large T-shirt shriveled in like a Shrinky Dink fresh out of the oven, and the rhinestones popped up as I tapped my finger where each one should be. They totally replaced the painted-on white logo.

When it was done, I was looking at the shirt of my dreams. *Project Runway*, watch out. The demonic designer was in the house!

As quickly as I could, I changed out of my boring, old T-shirt and into my brand-new rocker one. It was so awesome and the perfect fit. I could hardly believe I actually made it with my own powers. I felt so energized, I went right into my best Vale impression. I shook my hips, rocked out on air guitar, and sang the lyrics to Mara's Daughters' *Caught in My Web* at the top of my lungs. I was so into it that I didn't even notice my mom standing in my doorway until she spoke.

"I don't think so," she said. "Take that off this instant."

"Mom," I groaned. "Come on, it's not a big deal. Everyone in school will love it."

"No daughter of mine is leaving the house in something that tight and that revealing. Give me the shirt."

"But—"

"Don't but me, Angel." She put out her hand, and I gave her my prized possession. "You're way too young to go out in something like this."

That's what she thought. I made one shirt. I could just as easily make another.

Having powers had its advantages after all.

chapter

✧ 12 ✧

There was a whole crowd around Courtney on the steps at school on Wednesday morning. Even Cole was there. I pulled Gabi over to the side. "Watch this," I said. "But you have to block me."

Gabi raised an eyebrow, but I wouldn't give her any more details. She'd have to see this for herself. I was going to recreate the shirt I made the other night, and wow everyone. It would be perfect. Courtney would be totally jealous. And maybe, if Cole saw how amazing I looked, he'd forget about everything that happened before and like me again. It was a two-for-one.

"You're going to love this," I told Gabi as I waved my hands in front of my ugly pink and red striped T-shirt. I figured I might as well morph a shirt I already hated. Why lose a good one?

As I molded it into the rocker tee, I felt a slight breeze hit my skin. It was working. My black, one-shoulder shirt was almost ready for its Goode Middle School debut.

Gabi's eyes dropped to the ground. "Uhh, is that what you meant to do?"

I looked down. No. No. NO! I wasn't in a fabulous new shirt. I was in *no* shirt. NO SHIRT. Remember how embarrassed I was about that whole initial in the tree thing? Well, that was a happy, joyful memory compared to this. This was lock-yourself-in-the-janitor's-closet-and-refuse-to-ever-come-out humiliating. Because instead of making the coolest top in the universe, I made the one I was wearing vanish. I was now standing off to the side of school in my training bra. MY TRAINING BRA! AT. SCHOOL.

Shoot me now.

Gabi tried her best to block me, but the girl was a beanpole. She could only do so much.

"Forget something, Angel?" Courtney yelled over.

"Nice outfit," Jaydin butted in.

Everyone started laughing. I didn't look up. I didn't want to know if Cole was getting a good chuckle at my expense, too. My life was over. I had managed to survive the tree carving and the fireworks. No one bugged me about it, because unlike girls, boys don't really talk to their friends. But this? There was going to be no saving me from *this* humiliation. It was going to go down in Goode Middle School history. Angel Garrett: School Joke. And I deserved it. Why hadn't I just stuck with trying to move the pencil?

"She snagged her top on a branch," Gabi yelled back at them while I dug out my gym shirt and threw it on. "It tore, that's all."

I appreciated the attempt, but Gabi really needed to work on her lying. It was a pretty lame excuse and wasn't helping anything.

"You know," Courtney continued. "Training bras are for when you actually have something to train."

I could feel the heat in my cheeks. There was no doubt my face was now a lovely shade of stop sign red. My mind was a complete mess. I wanted to make some snippy comeback, but my brain could only manage one thought: Get away from these people. Now. So clad in the gym shirt, I raced past them and into school.

But I did manage to hear everything they said as I passed by.

"My day keeps getting better and better," Courtney gloated. "This was just the icing after the whole thing with D.L."

"I can't believe he's going to school here now," Jaydin said.

"Yep. He's living with his mom now, which means he's going to school in Goode. For everyone to see." I knew she added that last part for my benefit. She wanted me to know that D.L. was real.

"Too bad he missed this little show," Jaydin threw in. "I haven't laughed so hard in ages."

"No worries. I'm sure Double-A will strike again. A-cup Angel never fails to provide hours of entertainment," Courtney answered.

Was that going to be my name from here on out? *A-cup Angel?* My nonexistent chest was going to be the subject of hours, maybe years, of gossip and ridicule. Like I didn't have enough issues about it? Courtney was right. I did strike again. And once again, I managed to completely embarrass myself with my powers.

"Angel," Gabi said, following.

"No," I stopped her. "Just stay away from me. I'm dangerous."

"You're not," she said, chasing me down the hall. "It was just your powers mixing with your emotions. And Cole was standing right there."

"More reason to stay away from him."

"You were just doing something really advanced. And it didn't help matters that Courtney was there, too," Gabi said.

She wasn't making me feel better. "Yeah, perfect little Courtney." Courtney who always got everything she wanted. The girl who no one would ever dare make fun of. The one who would never be caught dead in front of her classmates topless! Nope, that only happened to people like me. "Now she even gets her boyfriend at school, too," I mumbled.

"How did that happen?" Gabi asked.

"Beats me. Prob—Oh. My. God."

Then another awful thought hit me. It was probably because of me that D.L was going to school with us. When I was fighting with Courtney yesterday, I had accused her of making her boyfriend up. I had said, "Let's see him. Bring him here."

Now it was actually happening. I was responsible for making Courtney's wish come true. Talk about unfair. How come my powers worked to help her dating life and ruin my own?

chapter
✧13✧

No way was I facing Cole and everyone else. So I marched straight to the nurse's office. I needed to be sent home. Pronto.

"What's wrong with you?" Miss Spring asked.

Other than death by embarrassment? Nothing. But I couldn't be honest with her. Miss Spring was the meanest, crotchetiest person in the whole building, and she didn't let anyone get away with missing class.

Allison Cheng had to throw up on her shoes last month before Miss Spring finally believed she was really ill and not just trying to get out of gym class.

"My head hurts and my stomach is all queasy. I think I may throw up." I added in that last part to remind her about Allison.

She studied my face and then handed me the

thermometer. "I'll be back." I knew she didn't believe I was sick. Although, after what just happened to me, I had to look awful. I certainly felt it.

I couldn't take any chances. I needed to be sent home. My first thought was to use my powers to make her think I was ill. But seeing as my voodoo was why I was in there in the first place, that didn't seem like the smartest idea. With my skills, I'd probably give myself mono or the plague or some mysterious deadly disease. So, I decided to play it safe and go the old fashioned way. I shoved the thermometer under the light bulb.

While I was waiting for it to heat up I picked up a copy of the morning announcements Miss Spring had left in the room. All the normal boring stuff like school sports scores were there, but what caught my attention were the very last lines. "Reminder: The school dance is just three weeks away. We're still looking for volunteers to be on the planning committee."

The school dance. I hadn't realized it was so soon. I really wanted to go. Well, I didn't want to just go. I wanted to go with Cole. But after everything that happened, my chances at winning the presidential election were probably better.

The clicking sounds of Miss Spring's shoes were getting closer. I shoved the thermometer back in my mouth and did my best not to let out a howl. The stupid thing burnt my tongue. The light bulb made it way too hot. I spit it out as Miss Spring walked in the room. "Here you go," I said, handing it to her. Although it came out more like, "Ha yuhh goww." My tongue had not healed yet.

"Are you going to call my mom now?" I asked, trying my best to sound normal.

She looked at the thermometer. "It looks like we're going to have to call the morgue. With a temperature like that, you must be dead." She pointed to the door. "Back to class."

Why did I leave it under the light for so long? Miss Spring stood there waiting for me to leave, but that wasn't an option. Begging, on the other hand, was. "Please, I can't go to class. Think of the most horrendous, horrifying, horrifically embarrassing thing that could ever happen in middle school, multiply it by ten, and then you have what happened to me. Please let me just sit here today. I'll go back tomorrow. I promise."

"Class, Angel," she said, handing me a hall pass.

The woman had no soul. How could she not cut me a break? "Please, I'll do anything. Just let me stay. Remember when you were in eighth grade. I'm sure there was a time someone helped you out. Come on, return the favor. Please."

"Go," she said.

I guess I knew what happened to the evil Courtneys of the world when they grew up. They turned into people like Miss Spring. After giving her the meanest look my face could twist itself into, I stood up and left the office.

Miss Spring could make me get out, but she couldn't make me walk fast. I went in super slow motion up the hall. As I was about to duck into the bathroom, the principal called out to me. "Miss Garrett, over here."

Busted. Absolutely nothing was going right.

I turned around to face Mr. Stanton and let out a small gasp. The guy standing by his side was stunning and, yet, somewhat familiar.

"Glad I ran into you," Mr. Stanton said. "I need to get to a meeting. Can you show this young man to his first class?"

I nodded. *Would I ever?* I mean, my heart still belonged to Cole, but this guy was a hottie. His eyes were almost magical.

"Great," Mr. Stanton said. "Angel Garrett meet D.L. Helper."

chapter

✦ 14 ✦

It was D.L. *The* D.L. *Courtney's* D.L. His Facebook picture did not do him justice. He was way better looking in person—tall, piercing eyes; hair that hung just the right way over one eye; and even a slight cleft in his chin. He could have been a model, except for maybe the chubby cheeks. But they didn't take away from his cuteness, they added to it. They made him seem approachable, friendly.

But I shouldn't have let his looks fool me. "You're . . . Angel?" he asked, giving me a simultaneous once over and sneer making me feel, once again, no better than a piece of gum stuck on the bottom of a shoe.

"Yeah," I said, wishing Mr. Stanton hadn't left me alone with him. I was getting the sinking feeling that D.L. and I weren't exactly headed toward bestfriendsville.

"Perfect," he said, swinging his backpack from his left to right shoulder. "Figures I'd get stuck with *you* on my first day." He started walking, leaving me standing there.

I'm not sure why I imagined he'd actually be a nice human being. Anyone who went out with Courtney had to have serious personality flaws. "Do you even know where you're going?" I called after him.

"I'll figure it out. Now get lost, please. I'd rather not be seen with you."

Well, Courtney obviously clued him in on my reputation at school. "Nice to meet you, too," I said, hoping he was smart enough to get the sarcasm.

I waited for some obnoxious comeback. But I didn't get one—not from him. Because the bell rang and we were right in front of a row of eighth grade homerooms. Courtney came running out and right into D.L.'s arms, giving him a huge hug.

"I'm soooo glad you're here," she wailed. When she finally let him go, she turned her attention to me. "Buzz off, Double-A. I don't need you and your gym shirt ruining this moment for me."

Big surprise. The new nickname was sticking. And while I was prepared for it, hearing her say it still made me cover my chest with my arms and slink backward.

"Jaydin, Lana, Bronwyn, Brooke," Courtney screamed out. "Come meet D.L."

She was so excited, and I was so . . . so . . . ready to give up.

As I headed down the hall, I tried to block out the whispers, giggles, and finger-pointing surrounding me, but I heard and saw everything. The more I cringed, the more they kept at it. The calls of "Double-A" and some not-so-flattering comments about my chest followed me as I walked. But they were overshadowed by Courtney's voice echoing down the hallway. She was obviously talking loud enough to guarantee I'd hear what she had to say to her friends. "I'm so excited about the school dance," she crowed. "And one of you is totally going to have to go with Cole. I hear he's looking for a new girlfriend."

My pulse sped up like someone shifted it into high gear. *Did she just say Cole!? With someone new? NOOOOO!!!*

As the voice in my mind screamed, every locker in the hallway burst open sending the contents shooting out onto the floor. Lou would have been impressed. I didn't just make one pencil move, I caused dozens of them, along with doors, papers, and books, to fly. Only I hadn't meant for that to happen.

People around me were shouting, but I could barely hear them over the sound of my heartbeat. Cole. *My* Cole was going to have a new girlfriend. How was I ever going to make it through the year if I had to watch as he made googly eyes at someone else? And, of course, Courtney would constantly rub my face in it, and now she had her boyfriend here to help her do it.

I moved through the books and other junk on the ground in a trance. There was nothing to do, other than go on with my hopelessly, pathetic, lonely existence. As I walked to class, my foot slid on a loose piece of paper causing me to fall right on my butt. If I wasn't so numb, it probably would have hurt. I just sat there on the ground looking at the damage I had caused. The hallway was a mess. Which was fitting.

So was my life.

chapter

✧ 15 ✧

Gabi stood with me while I waited in the cafeteria line. She never bought school lunch. Her mom didn't think it was nutritious enough. But she wasn't leaving my side. She was too afraid I'd have another freak out and destroy the whole school. Or zap the next person who called me Double-A into a dozen little pieces.

"Stay calm," she whispered to me. "Courtney doesn't know what she's talking about. She was just trying to mess with you. Cole isn't looking for a new girlfriend. He likes you."

"How can you say that? You know he doesn't. Not anymore. It's no wonder he's looking for my replacement." The lunch lady handed me my spaghetti and meatballs. "What am I going to do?"

"You're not going to *do* anything," she answered.

As usual, Gabi was right. I picked up a cup of

pudding and dropped it on my tray. Drowning my problems in chocolate was the only solution for now.

We headed for our table, but I stopped cold. Cole was standing in the middle of the cafeteria, at his table—the cool table—talking to Jaydin. Courtney hadn't been lying. Cole had moved on. He was over me and into someone new. A mean, gorgeous, popular someone new.

"It's probably nothing," Gabi said, putting her hand on my arm.

I shook my head. "No, it's something."

Then Brooke sat down and told Cole to come sit by her, and he did! What did that mean? I couldn't stop watching him. What was he doing with all these girls?

"Will you look at him?" I whispered hoarsely to Gabi.

"What? He sits there all the time," she said.

"This is different. Did you see that? He took some of Allison's chips and totally touched her hand. And the way he laughed when Bronwyn said something. Definitely flirting."

"You're reading *wayyyy* too much into this. You need to relax."

That was impossible. "He's probably asking one of them to the dance right as we speak."

"Angel," Gabi snapped, grabbing my pudding and

putting it back on my tray. It had floated an inch in the air.

The feeling I had when Lou got me so upset that I made the pencil fly across the room was back. It was the same one that stirred inside me when I caused the lockers to burst open. For once I knew my powers wouldn't fail me.

I looked up from the pudding. Then to Cole surrounded by girls.

Pudding.

Cole.

Pudding.

It was like the dessert was calling out to me. Not to eat it, but to shoot it across the room so it landed right in the middle of Cole's table. It would distract him. Make him stop smiling like he was at people who weren't me. Did I dare try? It wouldn't technically be doing anything wrong. It was just good old powers homework, and I needed the practice, right? The sooner I could learn to move objects, the sooner I could make everything okay with Cole again. That was all the convincing I needed.

After a quick look around to make sure the coast was clear, I made my move. With one sweeping motion to guide my powers, I sent the pudding sailing from my tray. Only it didn't land in the middle of the table. It had landed splat on Courtney's head.

Brown goop slid down her face. I did my best not to laugh as she let out a cry and wiped the pudding out of her hair. I hadn't meant for that to happen, but I wasn't going to complain. It seemed like justice to me.

I caught D.L. staring my direction. "It was Angel," he said to Courtney, loud enough for everyone to hear. "She threw it right at you."

"No, I didn't," I protested. "It was an accident. I never even touched the pudding." Which was technically true.

"I saw you do it," D.L. shot back at me.

"Oh? You saw me touch it with my hands? Did you? Did you?" There was no way he could have because I didn't use my hands. I used my powers. Then I realized that my no hands argument would draw attention to my "special gift." So as much as I didn't want to, I knew I had to give in to D.L. "Fine, I threw it."

That little announcement made Courtney stand right up, tray in hand. I had seen her mad before, but never this livid. Her eyes tiny slits, she put the tray in her right hand and flung it right at me. Spaghetti and meatballs tumbled through the air, with the tray landing right on Gabi's shoes.

"No way," Gabi screamed. "Not my suede Steve Maddens." She reached into her lunch bag. A Soylami sandwich wasn't exactly fling worthy, so she dumped it on the ground and pulled out her drink box. She shoved the straw in, aimed it at Courtney and squeezed.

A bright red stain the size of a plum formed in the middle of Courtney's shirt. The look on her face as she surveyed her shirt was scary enough to make flowers wilt. "Boy, are you are going to pay for this," she growled through clenched teeth.

"Food fight!" D.L. shouted. Seconds later the whole cafeteria erupted.

There was spaghetti, pudding, lettuce, granola bars, and an assortment of other foods whizzing throughout the cafeteria. I ducked for cover as a barrage of meatballs headed my way. I picked a slew of them up off of the ground and hurled them back at Courtney's table. My aim wasn't as good without using my powers, but I think I still managed to get her with a few. It was the most fun I had had in school in ages. Totally liberating. Even if I was now covered in tomato sauce. At least I only ruined my gym shirt. A lot of people were going to need to go shopping after today.

I was mid windup for my next meatball pitch when a voice filled the cafeteria. Using a bullhorn, Mr. Stanton declared, "Stop! Drop the food now."

chapter
✧ 16 ✧

"I want silence," Mr. Stanton said. No one said a word. He dropped his bull horn. He didn't need it anymore, no one was crazy enough to cross him when he was angry. "First the mess in the hallway and now this? I will not have this in my school."

He looked around, his eyes scanning the cafeteria, with occasional stops at some of the usual troublemakers. "I want to know who is responsible for this. Now."

Most people kept their heads down. I decided to step up, which was better than having D.L. or someone rat me out. "It was me," I said, taking a step closer to Mr. Stanton. "I started it."

"You?" he asked, giving me a look that made me feel the size of a Raisinette. "Why?"

I shrugged a shoulder and started biting my pinky nail. "Because . . . because . . . it was stupid." And it really was. It wasn't like my little stunt got Cole to stop thinking about other girls, or start liking me. All it did was get me in trouble. I really should have thought through the whole thing better.

"Let's go," he said. I was getting a personal escort to his office.

"It wasn't just her," Courtney chimed in. "Gabi started it, too."

"What?! That's not, you, uhh," Gabi stammered. Then she got it together and pointed a finger at her accuser. "It was her. Courtney's the one to blame."

Mr. Stanton took a deep breath. "All three of you come with me. And we might as well get to the bottom of this now. Who was the one who yelled 'food fight'?"

"Cole," D.L. said without missing a beat.

"Liar," I screamed. "It was you." He could not get away with messing with Cole. I wasn't going to stand for that.

"I don't know what she's talking about," D.L. said. "She's been trying to mess with me since you introduced us this morning." Then he turned his focus to me. "We're not in kindergarten anymore, Angel. If you like me, just say it. Don't try to pick a fight."

How dare he?! And in front of Cole? D.L. was rotten. But he was also an incredible liar. He sounded really convincing. I mean, I almost bought his story, and I knew for sure there wasn't any truth to it.

"I don't like you. I can't stand anything about you," I shot back.

"You know they say when someone protests too much, it's because they don't want to admit it's actually true," he said.

How was I supposed to respond to that? If I argued, I'd be protesting too much, and if I didn't, people might believe him. I hated D.L. Helper.

"Cole?" Mr. Stanton asked.

"I don't know if she likes him," he said, flicking pieces of spaghetti off of his shirt.

WHAT! How could he even think there'd be a possibility that I'd like that jerk over him. "I don't," I told Cole and everyone else in the room.

"That's not what I'm talking about," Mr. Stanton interrupted, shaking his head. "Were you the one who called 'food fight'?"

"No," he answered. Only he didn't tell on D.L. He was a better person that that.

"Quit lying," D.L. ordered. "You know you did it."

"Enough," Mr. Stanton stopped him. "You can both join me in my office. We'll figure this out there. The five of you—let's go."

chapter

17

"This is all because of you, Double-A," Courtney hissed at me, as we waited in the main office for Mr. Stanton to come give us our punishment. "You're so dead."

I ignored her. There were bigger things on my mind. For one, I was squished on a bench next to Cole who wouldn't look at me—just at the stupid ceiling. Cole who no longer liked me. Cole who had already moved on to other girls. Cole who I was still obsessed with. *Cole who had seen me in my training bra this morning.* Nothing Mr. Stanton would do could be a bigger punishment than I already suffered through.

But Courtney didn't let up. She went on with the name-calling, which led to her telling D.L. the whole story about me in my underwear, which led to D.L. making fun of me, too. "You didn't bother putting clothes on this morning? God, Garrett. You really are a spazz. What were you hoping, that flashing the school would—"

"Enough already," Cole finally opened his mouth.

I looked at him, but only out of the corner of my eye. I didn't trust myself to make full eye contact. Had Cole just come to my defense or was he just annoyed with D.L. and only now getting around to expressing it?

"What's your problem?" D.L. asked.

Cole clenched his fists. "Hmm . . . I wonder . . . Try you getting me in trouble for something I didn't do."

D.L. shrugged his shoulders. "Better you than me."

"You're lucky I didn't rat you out."

"Like that mattered." D.L. sneered at me. "Someone did it for you."

"Yeah, why didn't you tell on him yourself?" Gabi asked Cole. At least the conversation was steering away from my clothing malfunction.

"*I*," he said, glaring at D.L., "don't get other people in trouble."

D.L. didn't seem bothered at all. But Gabi and I—and even Courtney—looked uncomfortable. We had all pinned blame on someone. All of us but Cole. No one said another word until Mr. Stanton returned.

"Does anyone have anything to say?" the principal asked.

"I didn't do anything," D.L. protested.

I rolled my eyes.

"Well," Mr. Stanton said, "I have people here who say otherwise. And I just spoke to the lunchroom aides, and Mrs. Dill is positive that you not only called out 'food fight' but were the one who got her in the head with a meatball. Not the kind of first impression you want to make at a new school, young man."

I always knew I liked Mrs. Dill. D.L. kept his mouth shut after that.

"Cole, you can go," the principal said. Cole stood up and left which made me sad. Even though I knew I needed to stay away from him and was still mongo embarrassed about everything that happened, I still wanted to be near him.

Mr. Stanton interrupted my thoughts. "Your punishment," he said, looking us each in the eye, "is detention for the rest of this week and the next two weeks. Right up to the dance."

Gabi let out a gasp. I knew what she was thinking. Her mom was going to kill her. Gabi had a spotless record, which was expected in the Gottlieb house, anything less was met with lectures and many extra hours spent studying.

"I have Hebrew School on Tuesdays," Gabi said. "Although, I kind of wouldn't mind missing it," she threw in.

"You can be excused from detention that day," he told her.

"I have it, too," D.L. added.

"Why don't I call the instructor and get a list?" Mr. Stanton said. He was already onto D.L. and his games.

"Nah, that's okay," D.L. said. "I'm probably not on their list yet, anyway." Like he ever would be. I doubted he was even Jewish.

Then I realized something. If Gabi had Hebrew School on Tuesdays that meant I'd be stuck with Courtney and D.L. all by myself. That was cruel and unusual punishment and had to be fixed immediately.

"Mr. Stanton," I said, rising to my feet. "The others shouldn't have to pay for what I did. I'm the only one who should be punished."

"That's very nice of you to try and take all the blame, Angel, but you were not the only one involved in this," he said.

"But I *started* it. That's much worse. It's okay. Blame me." I didn't care if he expelled me. In fact, it sounded like the solution to most of my problems. No more jokes. No more teasing. I'd get to stay home. It would be like a vacation. Well, except for the part where my mother punished me for the rest of my life. Still, it beat being stuck in a room with Courtney.

"She makes sense," Courtney said, defying nature and agreeing with me for once.

"Yeah," I argued. "Courtney shouldn't have to serve detention. She's innocent."

"I know you're trying to help your friend, Angel," Mr. Stanton said, "but I'm not going to hear it."

"Courtney is *not* my friend," I said. "Ask anyone."

He ignored me. "You'll all start detention tomorrow. That way your parents can make arrangements to pick you up, if they need to. Now get to class."

That was it. There was no changing his mind. I was going to be stuck with Courtney and D.L. for two-plus long weeks.

chapter
✦ 18 ✦

An all too familiar scent wafted past me as I walked into my house. It was a vanilla, lavender, and mint combo. My mother's cleansing candles. She had them lit all over the house. She does this about once a month—to rid the house of negative spirits. But that's only half of it. After the candles are lit she takes her giant totem pole and shakes it in every corner of every room in the house. Apparently it's to scare ghosts away. Though if you ask me, she's more likely to be giving them a good laugh.

"Hey, Mom," I said.

"Angel," she said, swinging around so fast, I thought the totem pole was going to weigh her down and send her crashing. But she knew how to control the massive stick. "How was your day?"

"Good," I lied. "Just so you know, I'm going to stay after school for the next couple of weeks."

She and all the faces on the totem pole stared me down. "Why?"

"After school project."

She gestured for me to continue.

"Nothing exciting. Just an English assignment."

"What's it on?"

I stumbled for a second. All those eyes were making me nervous. *"Romeo and Juliet."*

"I love that play," she said. "What are you doing for it?"

"Umm, acting out a few scenes." I didn't want to lie to her, but I didn't want to tell her about detention either. She didn't know about my powers and leaving that part out made my actions seem a lot worse. After all, if it wasn't for my powers, I never would have set off the fireworks causing me to ignore Cole, which meant I never would have tried to alter my shirt to impress him, which meant I wouldn't have been humiliated, which meant Cole might still have wanted to date me—not someone else—and therefore there would have been no reason for me to send my pudding flying. So, ultimately, I really wasn't to blame for the food fight. My powers were.

"That sounds nice," Mom said. "I can quiz you on your lines later."

This was bad. I didn't have time to memorize Shakespeare. "That's okay. I got it under control. Besides, we're just putting it on for class. No parents allowed."

Mom and her stick moved closer to me. "Really?"

"Uh-huh," I bit the skin around my nails.

"Angel . . ." she said, drawing out my name.

"Yes?" I gave her a big smile, flashing my dimples.

"I know about the food fight. Mr. Stanton called me."

I should have known—that's why she was asking all the questions! It's just that I've never been in trouble before (or, more accurately, no one ever used to pay attention to me enough to notice) and neither has Ms. Perfect Attendance Gabi, so I never knew how the whole in-trouble-thing worked. Great. As if I weren't in enough hot water in all other areas of my life, now my mother had a case against me as well.

"What would possess you to do something like that?" She leaned the totem pole up against the wall, but it fell over, clunking to the floor. That did not help her mood. "Well?"

"Cole doesn't want to go out with me anymore

and he's been flirting with all these girls, and I got angry," I spit out. That part was true.

Mom took a few deep breaths, but they didn't seem to be calming her. She was probably freaked that I had started following in my father's evil footsteps. "That's not an excuse. You can't start fights every time you get angry."

"I know."

"Apparently, you don't." She took another breath. "First, a food fight, then lying to me. Up to your room, now."

Mom followed me up and collected my iPod, cell phone, and laptop. "You're to stay here and think about what you've done."

No problem there. She had all of my stuff. What else was there to do?

chapter
✦ 19 ✦

The only good that came out of the whole day (other than seeing Courtney with pudding on her face) was that I finally mastered moving an object forward. As I sat stuck in my room, I sent pencils, DVDs, jeans, and all the other junk on my floor sailing into a heap in the corner. It was actually kind of easy. I just had to remember how it felt to fling the dessert.

Lou popped in as I was sending a towel across the room. It ended up draped over his face. Served him right for arriving unannounced.

"Well done," he said, removing the towel. "I see you're ready for your next lesson. And I must add, nice job with the food fight. I am personally impressed."

I jumped off of my bed. "How do you know about that? You said you weren't going to spy on me at school."

He winked. "Don't worry. I wasn't there."

"Then how do you know about it?"

"I heard you telling your mother. You never said I couldn't spy on her." His light eyes got an extra bright glint to them.

Oh. Lou didn't know I used my powers for the food fight, he just thought I had been a good old-fashioned troublemaker. "Well, no spying on Mom, either. Leave her alone, you already messed her up enough." It was Lou's fault Mom was a new age groupie. When she found out she was married to the devil and not some college professor, she went a little loopy trying to find ways to ward him off.

"I told you before, I'd never hurt your Mom," he said, leaning against my dresser.

"You better not," I warned him. Not that I knew what I'd do if he went back on his word. It wasn't like I was any match for the devil, but still . . .

Lou pulled out his hPhone, checked it quickly, and returned it to his pocket. "Time for lesson two," he said, handing me a pencil. "You are going to stop this mid-flight."

That didn't sound too hard. I focused, sent the pencil flying—but it didn't stop. Not until it hit the wall.

"You'll get it," Lou assured me. "Keep practicing."

And then he was gone, leaving me there with another boring task.

I gave up on the exercise after sixteen more tries. My day was long enough, and it was my powers that got me in trouble in the first place. They were the absolute last thing I wanted to think about at the moment.

chapter
✦✦20✦✦

As I walked with Gabi to third period, Dana Ellers and Tracy Fine stopped right in front of us, interrupting our conversation. "Hey," Dana said.

"Hi," I said cautiously. I wasn't sure what she wanted, but my top guess was to make fun of me over flashing the school. That seemed to be every eighth-graders favorite hobby recently.

"Can't believe you reamed Courtney with that pudding. Totally awesome," she said. I was completely taken aback. Had my lunchroom escapades overshadowed my debut as an underwear model?

"Yeah," Tracy said, "It was about time someone..." Suddenly, Tracy bit her lip and Dana looked down. "We have to go." As quickly as that, the two of them scurried off.

It was pretty obvious why. Courtney had stopped

right behind me. And while my classmates may have liked seeing her taken down a notch, they weren't willing to publicly fess up to it. But it gave me hope. Maybe I wouldn't be Double-A forever.

"Just thought you'd like to know, I meant what I said. You're going to pay for messing with me." Courtney flipped her light hair over her shoulder. "I'm going to see to it that Cole finds someone way better than you."

Yes! That meant he hadn't asked anyone out yet! Maybe he wasn't over me any more than I was over him!

"Not only that," she continued. "I'm going to make sure he always remembers what a loser you really are. He's going to be begging people to forget he ever hung out with you. That's a promise."

"She's awful," Gabi said, stating the obvious, as Courtney walked away.

"I know," I said. "It's like nothing she does ever blemishes her record."

And then I had a thought. I pushed it down, but it kept bubbling to the surface. What if I gave her a blemish? And not on her record. The real kind that would ruin her perfect skin. I could give her the king of all zits right on the tip of her nose.

She'd finally feel what it was like to have people point and laugh. Sure, it involved using my powers. But it was for the greater good—to teach the mean girl a valuable lesson and make her a nicer person. It was the right thing to do. Very after school special.

I told Gabi my plan.

"That's not a good idea," she said. "You know what happens when you use your powers. Everything always goes wrong."

I knew this was way beyond my skill level, but I wanted to give it a try. "This is going to work. I can feel it," I reassured both Gabi and myself. And, sure, my powers had messed up a lot, but I did have luck that first time I morphed my T-shirt. I was due for them to work again. The odds were in my favor. Kind of like flipping a coin. If you did it enough eventually you were bound to land on tails.

Gabi rubbed her temples. But I knew this was the answer. My emotions were primed for a Courtney payback. I closed my eyes and pictured Rudolph the Red Nose Reindeer's nose superimposed over Courtney's. "Make it a huge zit," I whispered over and over. I could see it, almost feel the massive pimple rising to the surface. When I was sure I must have succeeded, I turned to Gabi and gloated. "I think I got it this time. I just have this funny feeling. Wait until you see the zit. I bet it's scary."

"I know it is," she said, reaching into her purse.

"How? Courtney's nowhere around here."

"Don't say I didn't warn you." She pulled out a compact mirror and held it up to my face.

I pinched myself just to see if I was asleep. It had to be a bad dream—it just had to be. Because right there on the tip of my nose was a pimple big enough to make the *Guinness Book of World Records*.

chapter

✦ 21 ✦

With my head down, I took a seat next to Gabi in detention. All morning I had been trying to get rid of the monster living on my face, but it wouldn't go away. That zit had dug itself into my skin and wouldn't budge. It not only made me look like a fool, but it royally messed up my plans to get back at Courtney.

It also meant that now more than ever there was no way I could go near Cole. He couldn't see me looking this way. No one could.

"I'll be in the teachers' room," Miss Simmons, the school's new science teacher, said, when D.L., the last of the lunchroom riot detainees arrived. "I expect you all to behave."

When she was gone, D.L. stood up. "Let's get out of here. Do something fun until she gets back."

"No way," Gabi said. "I'm in enough trouble

already." I thought my mom was mad, but it was nothing compared to Gabi's. Mrs. G was a major perfectionist and having her daughter involved in a school scandal did not sit well with her. Not only did Gabi get a mongo lecture last night and have to write a letter to the lunch aides apologizing for the mess she helped make, but all weekend, her mom was going to make her do every chore she could dream up. And knowing Mrs. G that would be a whole lot of work. All that in addition to the detentions. It stunk.

"Lame," D.L. said.

"We're not *The Breakfast Club*," Gabi shot back.

"The what?" Courtney asked.

"Some eighties movie. A bunch of kids stuck in detention together. They don't like each other but end up running around the school and sharing secrets. By the end, they're all friends," she explained.

That certainly wasn't going to happen here. There wasn't even a slight chance that Courtney and I would bond over getting in trouble.

"Whatever," D.L. said and sat back down.

"No one's stopping you from leaving," I muttered, my face leaning down on my desk.

"Right. And have you run and tell Miss Simmons? No, thanks."

"Seriously," Courtney chimed in. "She would tell in a heartbeat. You can't trust her at all. I actually tried to be friends with her once. But she totally betrayed me. Even ditched me at my own party."

That wasn't what happened. She made me choose between my best friend or being a part of her group. I chose Gabi. After that, there was no way I could stick around for the rest of Courtney's party. I wasn't welcome.

Her story was interrupted by the door swinging open. I did a double take and every bit of me froze. It was Cole. What did he want? Why was he in detention? I had to make sure to keep my nose covered.

"Perfect timing," Courtney practically sang. "I was just telling D.L. how humiliating it was when Angel ditched me. One minute she acts like she's your friend, and the next she's ignoring you," she said, trying to make me look like the bad guy in front of Cole. I was so upset, I could even feel the zit on my nose burning. "It's just cruel. Right, Cole? I mean, she did that to you, too, right?"

How dare she? "It's not like that," I said, slapping my desk.

"Whoa," Courtney said, her laugh starting off

small and erupting into a full-fledged cackle. "Are you hatching something on your face?"

I had been covering my nose with my hand but Courtney's comment made me so angry I stopped without realizing it. My hand swung back up to my nose. But by that time it was too late. Everyone saw it. *Everyone.* Including Cole. That was not supposed to happen. Now he'd picture me like that forever, some Bozo the Clown reject. I considered taking a nosedive out the window. If nothing else, the zit might have burst from the impact.

"I want to disappear," I said under my breath. I needed to disappear. And before I knew it, I *did* disappear.

chapter

✦ 22 ✦

It was the weirdest thing, watching my body fade in front of my own eyes. It became almost translucent until it wasn't there at all. And yet, I was. I could see everything. Courtney jumping out of her seat. Cole grasping his neck and stuttering in confusion, D.L. staring at me, or at the chair I'd been sitting in, and Gabi stumbling around. She took her desk and flung it upside down. I had to give her credit, causing a distraction was quick thinking.

"Where'd she go?" Courtney asked, moving in my direction.

I ran past her to the closet, accidentally bumping into her as I went. She rubbed her shoulder. She had felt that. It was like I was still there—just not.

It wasn't like I could float through air or anything. I was still me. Only no one could see. But unless I could make myself reappear soon—and not in front of them—I'd have some serious questions to answer. Quietly as I could, I opened the closet door and snuck inside. No one seemed to notice, all their eyes were on Gabi.

"She just vanished," I heard Cole say.

"No, she didn't," Gabi replied.

"Then what happened to her?" he pressed on.

"She's just, umm, just, she's . . . uh, she ran out."

I tuned out the conversation and Gabi's attempts to explain my disappearance. I needed to focus on making myself visible again.

Body come back, I silently ordered. *And without the zit.* Nothing. I was still a ghost. If Gabi wasn't struggling so much trying to cover up, I wouldn't have minded staying that way for a bit. To think of all the amazing things I could have done. Spied on Cole. Hid all of Courtney's clothes during gym—leaving her nothing but her gym outfit. Made D.L. look like—

"I'm sure Angel will be back any second," Gabi yelled, interrupting my fantasy.

Focus Angel. Gabi needs you. "Body return. Body return. Body return," I whispered.

Ever so slowly, it started happening. First, I was a faint outline, then it started to fill in, the color

115

returning to my arms, legs, and clothes. I reached up and felt my nose. The pimple was still there, too. I contemplated staying hidden, but I knew I couldn't.

"Hi," I said, pushing the closet door open.

Everyone turned around to look at me.

"My God. I think your pimple grew in the last three minutes. What were you doing in there, anyway?" Courtney gestured at the closet. "Trying to run away from it?"

"Mouse," I answered. "I saw one run across the floor, and I ran for the closet. They freak me out."

"Yeah." Gabi nodded. "That's why I knocked over the desk. I saw it, too."

"Eww," Courtney groaned, stepping up on her chair and searching the ground beneath her.

"But you just vanished," Cole insisted, his eyes right on me. "I didn't see you run anywhere." He must have been really freaked out to forget that he wasn't speaking to me.

I put my hand back over my nose. I didn't like him looking at me with that thing there. "I'm fast."

"Not that fast," he said, running his fingers through his curls. "You just disappeared."

"Don't be a moron," D.L. butted in. "How could she just disappear?"

"I don't know," Cole said, leaning against the doorframe, looking deep in thought.

"Everything happened really quickly," Gabi said, trying to make him feel better. "I didn't see her run off, either."

"But—"

Gabi cut him off and tried to change the subject. "Are you stuck in detention, too?"

"No, I just needed to ask Courtney something."

He walked over to her desk and whispered. Both Gabi and I strained to hear. "Did you start that huge science questionnaire?" he asked.

"Yeah," Courtney said.

"Any way you want to lend it to me?" he asked giving her one of his cute, lopsided grins. "I haven't even started and there's no way I'll get it all done by Monday. Not without staying in the entire weekend."

D.L. didn't seem to like what Cole was saying at all, which surprised me, because I totally pictured him as a cheater. "Do it yourself," he snapped. But maybe he was just jealous that someone as cute as Cole was asking his girlfriend for a favor.

"Angel can help you," Gabi offered. I looked over at her to make sure I hadn't accidentally erased her mind again. This was definitely not Gabi. First, she hated copying. She thought it was dishonest. Second, I was supposed to be avoiding Cole, not figuring out ways to talk to him. And third, I barely had any of the homework done, either.

"That's okay," Cole told her.

Still, the idea that he'd rather flunk than deal with me was disheartening. Was it because he couldn't stand the idea of being around me? Or was he embarrassed at the thought of hanging out with the walking zit?

"Yeah," Courtney said. "Besides, there are tons of people who would help him. I bet Jaydin or Brooke would be happy to."

I didn't want that. And while I knew better, I opened my mouth to speak. "No, it's no problem. Gabi and I are meeting on Sunday at Goode's Greatest Pizza to go over it. You should join us."

"Okay," he said, half-heartedly.

"What is going on in here?" Miss Simmons demanded when she walked into the room and saw Gabi's toppled desk. "I should be able to leave a group of eighth-graders alone without chaos breaking loose."

"I should go," Cole said slinking toward the door.

"Five o'clock," Gabi called after him.

That Gabi is some operator. In the midst of getting reamed by Miss Simmons, she still managed to nail down plans with Cole.

"Out," Miss Simmons said to Cole. Then she looked back at us. "Since you can't behave, during your next detention I'll find a project to keep you all busy. How does that sound?"

"Just perfect," D.L. muttered. "We can thank Garret for getting us into even more trouble."

Courtney rolled her eyes at me.

"It wasn't me. It wasn't anybody," I tried to explain to Miss Simmons. "A mouse ran right over my feet. That's what caused all the problems."

Miss Simmons scowled. "I'll have the office call an exterminator. This day just keeps getting worse."

Maybe for Miss Simmons it was getting worse, but for me it was getting a million times better. Cole was still willing to hang out with me. Maybe he didn't hate me after all. Or maybe he was just desperate for help with his homework, but still, it was something. And while I was probably going to be stuck collating science packets or whatever odd job Miss Simmons came up with for the next two weeks, at least she made everyone forget about my disappearing. The day was definitely getting better.

chapter 23

The excitement over getting to hang out with Cole disappeared as Gabi and I headed home. "How am I supposed to help him with his homework when I'm supposed to be staying away from him? I can't do both at the same time. You never should have volunteered me."

Gabi stopped dead in her tracks. "It makes no sense for you to still be ignoring Cole."

"Of course it does," I told her. What was wrong with her today? "You know why I'm doing it."

"Yeah, why?"

I rolled my eyes. "Because my powers tend to go off around him."

"They've been doing that, anyway," Gabi reminded me. "He was there when you erased everyone's memories and disappeared into thin air. It can't get

120

much worse than that. And you're just adding to it by pretending he doesn't exist."

"But what if something else happens? Like a repeat of the fireworks or our initials in a tree. Something specifically having to do with him. He'll think I'm a freak."

"He already does," she said under her breath.

"What?"

She shrugged her shoulder. "You've been acting crazy around him, and he's definitely noticed. So you might as well talk to him. Maybe it will actually make things better."

I chewed on my nails as I contemplated what she said. My plan had definitely been backfiring. The whole point of keeping away from him was to protect him from my deranged powers. But he was still affected by them. And he still saw every single embarrassing situation that I accidentally conjured up.

"You're right." Trying to ignore Cole didn't do anything but make him think I was crazy *and* rude.

"I know," she said. "That's why I told him you'd help him. You'll get a chance to make things right. And I'll be there, to keep you from doing anything too stupid."

"Yeah, because that's been working out really well." She hadn't been able to stop my T-shirt from disappearing, the zit from popping up, or me disappearing into thin air.

She shrugged a shoulder. "At least I've helped you make up harebrained excuses."

That was true. She really was an amazing friend. "You don't think it's too late? That I blew it with him completely?"

"No way," Gabi assured me. "He liked you before, he'll like you again. You haven't been ignoring him *that* long. Just make sure you're extra nice to him from now on."

That was exactly what I was going to do. From there on out, I was going to put on the charm, and finally make my dream come true—Cole and Angel together forever.

But first I had to get rid of the baseball perched on top of my nose.

chapter
✦ 24 ✦

It took six hours, more concentration than I knew was possible, and a series of blunders like making my whole face break out into polka dots (I looked like a bag of wonder bread), but I finally managed to get rid of the mongo zit that inhabited my face. And it was a good thing, too. Because there was no way I was meeting Cole looking like that.

"I can't believe I'm actually going to hang out with him again," I said to Gabi as we rode our bikes to Goode's Greatest Pizza on Sunday. "Thank you so much. This would not be happening without you."

"I know," she said and laughed. "It even made you do your homework."

"Seriously." But my sunny mood soon clouded over.

"Look who it is!" Courtney headed straight toward us. "Tweetle Dee and Tweetle Dumb."

"What do you want?" I asked. I wished Gabi hadn't said what time we were meeting Cole in front of Courtney. I should have known she'd show up.

"Oh, Double-A, your memory must be as small as your chest. I warned you. You messed with the wrong girl. I'm here to remind Cole what a disappointing embarrassment you are."

"Whatever," I said, and walked passed her with Gabi following close by.

"Oh, you might want to hurry. Jaydin is already in there helping him with the homework."

I stopped short. "What?"

"That's right," she said. "Cole doesn't need your help anymore. He found someone way better." With that she turned on her heels and walked inside.

"I have to get in there," I said, taking a step forward, but Gabi grabbed onto me.

"Whoa," she said. "You need to calm down first. If you go in there like this, who knows what will happen."

She made perfect sense, but I didn't care. Cole was supposed to be studying over pizza with me, not Jaydin. I had to separate them pronto. If I didn't, any chance of me having a relationship with Cole was done for. There was no way freak show, Double-A Garrett could compete with beautiful, I-can-have-any-guy-I-want Jaydin. "My God, they're probably in love already. Just sitting there having some spectacular old time." I tried to relax, but I couldn't. I was feeling too sorry for myself. "It's not fair. I should be the one having an out of this world evening—not *her*."

"You still can," Gabi said. "Cole made plans with you. He won't ditch you."

I hoped she was right, but I wasn't so sure. I tried to control my emotions, but my insides were swirling. I closed my eyes and took some cleansing breaths. It wasn't working.

"What is that?!" Gabi exclaimed.

I opened one eye to peek. Then the other to make sure I wasn't seeing things. A small tornado was barreling right toward us. I grabbed Gabi by the wrist and ran. She staggered an arm's length behind me.

"Go," Gabi said, gasping for breath. "Get away from it. I can't run in these shoes."

"I'm not leaving you."

We darted for a nearby tree and ducked down, our hands over our heads. The funnel engulfed us, making everything go silent. Then we began to tumble. I lost track of Gabi in the haze. I called out to her but heard nothing, not even the sound of my own voice.

Seconds later, the tornado was gone. But I was no longer huddled beneath a tree. I was way above it. Way, way above it. I was in outer space.

I maintained my own calm for a whole eighth of a second, and then I let out a massive scream that echoed all around me and reverberated inside of the astronaut helmet I was now wearing, making it hard to concentrate. I was in *outer space*!!!

But I had to get a hold of myself. I needed to get home. Pronto. I focused on the pizza joint the best I could and prayed with all of my might to return there safely.

"Please powers, kick in."

They didn't. This was bad. I was stuck in space. A big, black empty abyss. Floating hopelessly in the dark with no way home. What if this was my future—to drift aimlessly forever? My mom would always wonder what happened to me. And Gabi. She'd probably—Gabi!

I completely forgot about her. Where was she? I saw her get sucked into the funnel. She *had* to be nearby. I looked to the left, right, downward, but she was nowhere. My pulse quickened. Had the galaxy swallowed my best friend? Would I ever see her again? My eyes burned. The tears were coming, and I didn't even try to stop them. I made my only real friend disappear into the black hole of Space.

"Gabi!" I yelled. "Gabi! Where are you?"

Nothing.

I was panicked. What was I supposed to do? Not that it really mattered. Without Cole or Gabi, what really was there left for me?

Just as I was about to let myself float off aimlessly, I heard a squeal coming from above me. I looked up, and my tears gushed out even harder than before. Only this time it was because I was relieved. Gabi was hovering about thirty feet above me. Thank goodness!

She was trying to say something, but I couldn't hear her through the helmet. I figured she was light years away.

"What?" I called to her, trying to stay in one place. It was a challenge since I was weightless and drifting. I tried not to hyperventilate. If I passed out, there was no telling where I'd fly off to.

Gabi waved both hands around her and kicked with her feet. She looked like she was swimming the breast stroke. She did it until she reached me. At least we were together now. We could help each other figure out how to survive this nightmare.

"This is the coolest thing ever," Gabi shouted, then proceeded to do three back flips.

"Cool? That is so not the word for this," I snapped. Why wasn't she freaking out? My momentary relief of finding her was gone and replaced by the realization that I had no idea how to get us home. "This is serious. What if we're stuck here for days? There's nothing to eat. We could drift off to who knows where—"

Gabi started giggling. "Maybe we can make friends with some aliens, and they'll invite us for dinner."

The atmosphere must have been messing with her brain. This was no laughing matter.

"Gabi, get yourself together," I shouted as she pirouetted and leaped around me. "We have to figure out how to get home."

"Do we *have* to?"

"Gabi!"

"Fine," she said, while somersaulting. "I'll help you. But can't we have a little fun first?" Sometimes that girl totally baffles me. She'll freak out about a B-minus on a quiz, a broken nail, and watching scary movies, but send her to outer space and she felt right at home.

"No," I said. There was no time for fun. Getting back to Goode was the only thing that mattered.

Gabi ignored me and leaped higher up into the stratosphere. Each jump was ten feet high. She did it twelve times before landing next to me. "You've got to try this," she said. I could see her grinning through the helmet, and before I knew it she gave me a push, sending me drifting off.

"Stop!" I shrieked, fighting against the atmosphere to return to her side. "What are you doing?"

"Come on," she urged me. "You need to have fun, too. Just give it a try."

I didn't care how impressive her back flips looked, I was not taking part in space acrobatics.

"Take us back to Goode, take us back to Goode." I kept repeating it until my voice went hoarse. "My powers won't reactivate."

Gabi air cartwheeled over to me. "I bet I can jump-start them," she said.

"Then do it!"

She got a wicked little smile on her face. "Okay, but first you have to have a little fun. This is too cool. You can't go back home without at least playing a little. Just try—for me?"

"I don't want to."

"Come on," she coaxed me. "Don't you want my help to get us back? A few minutes of fun, that's all I'm asking."

She didn't play fair. "Fine." So, with hopes that my peanut butter and jelly sandwich from lunch wouldn't make a reappearance, I decided to give space gymnastics a try.

I tumbled, belly flopped, and even picked Gabi up by my baby finger and tossed her higher into the atmosphere.

Gabi spiral dived down to me. "See, wasn't that awesome? Aren't you glad you didn't waste this opportunity?"

"You sound like your mom," I told her.

Gabi shrugged her shoulder. "Even my mom is right once in awhile. Now come on, didn't you have fun? Even a little?"

"Fine. It was kind of cool to be able to do a quadruple flip, but I really want to go back now. Are you going to help me?"

"Here's what I'm thinking," she said after squeezing in a few more somersaults. "Since we got up here when you were talking about an *out of this world* time," she reasoned. "Maybe now we should talk about having a *Goode* time."

Was she really making puns at a time like this? "That's your big plan? That won't work. Besides I was angry when I talked about an out of this world time."

"You seem pretty angry now," Gabi said, falling backward to do the back float.

Oh. That Gabi was smart.

Then she started calling me names like Double-A and Freak Show, but coming from her it just made me laugh.

Then she hit a nerve. "If we don't get back home, you're just giving Cole more time to hang out with Jaydin. They're probably kissing right now."

OH. MY. GOD. Our little space odyssey made me forget about Cole. I stood him up, with Jaydin right there to take my place. Why hadn't Gabi reminded me earlier? I definitely need to get back. Now.

"I wonder if he'll think she's a better kisser than you," she went on. "Oh, that's right. He doesn't even remember your kiss."

I knew she was just saying these things to get me worked up, but it still really bothered me. "Stop it, Gabi," I said, my temper flaring up.

"Nope. They're probably k-i-s-s-i—"

She didn't get to finish spelling it out. Because

131

right in the middle, the tornado appeared and headed straight for us. It grabbed hold of both Gabi and me and hurled us right back where we had started—the tree near Goode's Greatest Pizza.

"I'm sorry," Gabi said, rubbing her head. She had bumped it during the landing. "I only said all those things because I knew it would get us home."

I didn't even answer her. I just ran into the restaurant. Cole was nowhere to be seen. I looked at the clock. Eight o'clock—I was three hours late.

I headed over to my bike. I needed to get home before Mom had a fit. She only let me out because I said it was for a school project.

Gabi followed me. "You know I didn't mean what I said up there, right?"

I nodded.

"Everything's going to be okay," she assured me.

But somehow, it really didn't seem that way.

chapter ✦ 25 ✦

I got to homeroom early Monday hoping I'd get a chance to talk to Cole. I had called him twice on Sunday night to apologize for not showing up, but the call went straight to voicemail both times.

The minute he got to his desk, I blurted out, "I'm so sorry."

He didn't even turn around.

"Cole," I said. "Please. Things got crazy. I didn't mean to leave you stranded."

He shifted to face me. "You could have at least texted."

"I was out of range." He had no idea how far! "Otherwise I would have."

"Whatever," he said, and turned back around. "I should have expected it from you."

There was silence. What could I say to that? His

words made me feel awful. "You can still look at my science homework if you want," I said, my voice less than a whisper.

"No thanks," he said. "Did it without you."

I wanted to know if that meant he did it on his own, or with Jaydin's help, but there was no way I could ask that.

When the bell rang, he left without as much as a glance at me. It was like that all day.

As I headed to detention with Gabi, we passed about a dozen signs for the dance. Like I needed another reminder that I didn't have a date and would probably never ever have one again.

"He's never going to take me to the dance now," I complained.

"I don't have anyone to go with, either," Gabi said. I didn't want to seem unsympathetic, but that didn't make me feel better.

I slumped into my desk in detention and stared straight ahead. I just wanted to go home.

"Let me have your attention," Miss Simmons said. "I've reached a decision. Since we need more volunteers for the dance's planning committee"— she looked at all of us—"I'm appointing all of you. You can come up with a theme, be in charge of decorations, come up with a prize for the king and queen. Now get to it."

D.L. let out a groan. I felt the same way. The dance was the last thing I wanted to think about.

Miss Simmons didn't seem to care what we thought. She just left for the teachers' room with a warning not to cause any trouble or we'd be spending the rest of the year sitting in her classroom after school.

"I don't want to be on some stupid dance committee," D.L. moaned.

We were on the same page. Neither did I.

"It'll be fun," Courtney said, her face lighting up. "We get to create the perfect night. Something really romantic. I'm sure Jaydin will thank us."

Courtney looked right at me. "Did you hear? Cole asked her to the dance. Right after you ditched him at the pizza shop." She tried to look all innocent. "I hope I didn't have anything to do with that."

As Courtney watched my expression, she looked like someone told her she'd never have to do another drop of homework her entire life. I wanted to scream at her. *You're lying. It's not true.*

Only I knew it was. Living in outer space was looking much more appealing.

chapter

26

You are not going to cry. You are not going to cry. I hoped my tear ducts would obey.

"How about a Hollywood/Oscars theme for the dance," Gabi said, trying to change the subject. Once again she came through for me, diverting attention to give my pink watery eyes an opportunity to clear up. "We could have a red carpet, people snapping pictures like the paparazzi, stars hanging on the walls. It could be totally cool."

"Lame," Courtney said. But I knew she was just saying that because it was Gabi's idea. She had to be salivating over the thought of acting like a celebrity. She pretended to be one every day of the week.

"What do you guys think?" Courtney asked me and D.L.

"It doesn't matter," I muttered, my face staring out

the window. I didn't dare look at any of them for fear my eyes would start leaking.

"Of course it matters," Courtney objected. "Don't you want the perfect backdrop, so everyone can see how cute Cole and Jaydin are together?"

Typical, horrible Courtney. Making sure she rubbed Cole's new girlfriend in my face.

"Anyway," Gabi answered for me. "What are your ideas?"

"I know," D.L. said. "We should do something like a haunted house. We could all dress up as something evil. Garrett would make a killer she-devil."

Did he just say what I think he said? OH. MY. GOD. He knew. For a second my thoughts about Cole were trumped. Somehow D.L. figured out my secret. "I AM NOT THE DEVIL," I blurted out. "Why would you think that? I'm just like everyone else. Tell 'em, Gabi."

My breathing got superfast. This was disastrous. Of all the people to find out, it couldn't be him! He'd totally blackmail me, rat me out to a gossip magazine, call the FBI, something. Then it hit me how stupid I was being. There was no way D.L. could have known. My breathing slowed back down, but not in time to escape Courtney's ridicule.

"Whoa," she said. "Somebody's in extra freak show mode today." Then she stood up. I knew what that meant—she was about to do one of her nasty imitations. "I AM NOT THE DEVIL." She had my voice down, but added in her own flare with her arms waving in the air and running in a circle.

D.L. cracked up. "Yeah, seriously, Garrett, why so defensive?" He looked at me like I just drank the formaldehyde used to preserve the frogs for dissection.

"Maybe she just doesn't like to be called the devil," Gabi responded.

"Then maybe," he replied, "she shouldn't go getting everyone in trouble and stuck in detention."

So that was it. I was right. He didn't really know I had devil genes, he was just annoyed with me. It was all a scary coincidence with D.L. being his usual irritating self.

"You're just as much to blame as I am," I said.

"Hardly. You brought everything on yourself."

The sad part was—he was right. Everything wrong with my life was one hundred percent my doing. Why did I ever think ignoring Cole was a good idea? If I had just talked to him after the whole fireworks thing maybe we'd still be together now.

Miss Simmons came back into the room and dismissed us. I could not get out of the room fast enough.

"You really lost it in there," Gabi said, following me home. "There was no way D.L. could have known about your dad. Then you went and almost told him. You need to keep yourself from overreacting to everything."

I stopped walking and turned around to face her. "Overreacting? I think I'm entitled to overreact. Cole is completely over me. He even asked someone else to the dance."

"He only did that because he thought you had given up on him," she said, twirling a strand of her light brown hair around her finger. "You just have to show him that you didn't. Try and get him back."

"Right. Like he's gonna ditch Jaydin to go out with me." I started walking again.

Gabi had to run to keep up with me. "He asked you out before. He could have chosen her then, too. But he didn't."

That was true. He actually did like me . . . once.

"But that was before I got all weird."

She didn't even know what to say to that, because it was true. After a long pause, she finally spoke.

"So un-weird yourself. Step up your training with Lou, and go out of your way to make things better with Cole. Make him see you're still the same girl you were before."

Gabi was right. I couldn't let Jaydin win. I could get Cole back. I just needed to fight for him.

So the next day in homeroom, I gave him my absolute brightest smile when he took his seat. "Hi, Cole."

"Hi," he answered, keeping his back to me. At least he didn't totally ignore me.

"Thanks again for having me over to watch the Mara's Daughters video." I know it was a lame attempt at conversation. He had me over a lifetime ago. But I really didn't know what to say, and I hoped reminding him that we had been on a date would make him wish we were going on another one. Only it didn't seem to be working. Maybe that date just reminded him of how crazy and embarrassing I had acted. I was going to have to go another route.

"Sure." His back was still to me.

Ughh. The one word answers were killer. Now I know how he must have felt when I avoided him. It was time for me to be bold. "So I was thinking," I said, trying to muster up some courage. "That maybe we could grab some pizza after I finish detention today. You know, to make up for the other day."

I had never asked someone out before. It was scary. The seconds he took before he answered felt like millenniums. "Can't. Hebrew School today."

"Oh, that's right." Duh. I should have known that. I felt foolish, but I pushed forward, anyway. "Maybe some other time then?"

"Maybe."

He might as well have said, "I'd rather take a math test while submerged in ice water with snakes biting my toes than hang out with you," because that's how it felt.

Cole had moved on. But I wasn't giving up. That just meant I was going to have to come up with some other way to get through to him.

chapter

✧ 27 ✧

Courtney took D.L.'s hand in detention and giggled at everything he said. D.L. kept whispering things in her ear which just made her even more giddy. It was a little puke-inducing actually. But while watching them act all couple-y was bad, having them turn their attention to me was much, much worse.

"What freak show behavior do you have in store for us today, Double-A?" Courtney sneered. "Gonna throw a hissy fit, wet your pants, *cry* over Cole?"

D.L. laughed.

I felt like Little Red Riding Hood right before the wolf pounced and gobbled her up. "Let's just finalize a theme for the dance," I said, trying to ignore the taunts, "before Miss Simmons gets back."

"We're going to do Under the Sea," Courtney said matter-of-factly.

"Says who?"

"Says me."

She was so smug, I just couldn't let her get her way, even though I really didn't care. "No. I think we should have a luau."

"That's dumb," Courtney snapped at me. "I am not going to a dance with a bunch of people in Hawaiian shirts. It's tacky. With my idea, everyone can dress up."

"As what—a fish?"

Her eyes narrowed in on me. "What do you care, anyway? It's not like *you* have a date."

She is not going to get to you. She is not going to get to you. She is not going to get to you. I clutched hold of my desk to try and calm myself. "So what? I still have a say."

"Well, we outnumber you." Courtney reached over and took D.L.'s hand.

He shrugged his shoulders at me. "She's right."

"I have Gabi's vote," I said.

"And I have *Cole's*," she shot back.

I was now grasping the desk so tight, I was afraid I was going to tear a piece of it off. "He's not even part of the committee!"

But she knew that. She just wanted to get under my

skin. And it was working. It felt like she plucked every little hair out of my arms with tweezers. "Let's just wait for Miss Simmons. She can be the deciding vote."

"She's not going to care," D.L. added, still holding Courtney's hand. "She'll just make us decide."

"So Under the Sea it is," Courtney declared.

"Hawaii," I fought back.

"Under. The. Water." She stood up to tower over me.

I jumped to my feet, too. "Hawaii."

"UNDERWATER!"

"HAWAII!"

And suddenly, we were in what had to be Hawaii. There was no tornado, no vortex thing this time. Just a flash.

But we weren't on the mainland. We were out in the water on surfboards.

A big wave was approaching. We were about to be *underwater* in *Hawaii*.

chapter

28

Courtney let out a scream so loud, I would have heard it even if I was still in outer space. I felt like joining in, but I kept my cool. Sort of. While I may not have been screaming on the outside, I was certainly doing it on the inside. This was not in my plans. I certainly didn't want to be in Hawaii. Especially not with my worst enemy and her boyfriend.

"Calm down," D.L. yelled out over Courtney's shriek. "And focus. That's the only way to get out of this."

At least one of us was keeping their cool. And even though D.L. was a jerk, he was also right. I needed to focus.

"Just center yourself and do it," he went on.

A little weightlessness sure would have come in handy right about then. I was having a hard time balancing on the surfboard. I took a deep breath.

"That's right," D.L. encouraged. "Now concentrate on your goal."

"Okay. Center." Wait, what? If I didn't know better, I would have thought D.L. was on to me. But that was impossible, wasn't it? Either way I had more crucial things to focus on—like stopping the wave before it killed us. I did not want to be fish food. Why hadn't I practiced Lou's lessons more? If I had learned to stop the pencil midair, I probably would have been able to stop the wave. The two seemed pretty similar.

I held my breath as water splashed all around us. But it went right up my nose causing me to gasp for air. The water got in my mouth making me have a coughing fit. If I didn't do something soon, the wave was going to overtake me.

"You can do this," D.L. yelled. "I know you can."

"What?!" Okay, he was freaking me out. Did he know?

It didn't matter. I was going to take the advice, anyway. I could do this. I had to. Otherwise we were all dead meat.

I focused my energy on the wave. I even pushed my arms out, but the wave kept coming. I gathered up all the strength I possessed. "Stop," I screamed.

And it did. The wave didn't move any farther. It

slowly cascaded down into the rest of the water as I dropped my arms. Everything was calm. Except for my mind, that is. It was still racing from what just happened and the thought that D.L. was somehow onto my secret.

"See, you did it," he said wrapping his arms tight around Courtney. They were on the same surfboard. "You stayed calm and you didn't fall into the water. You're going to make a great surfer."

Then I realized. D.L. wasn't onto my powers. He hadn't been trying to help me. I had misunderstood. He had been talking to Courtney the whole time, trying to get through the whole ordeal. He probably didn't even remember I was there. Figured.

Courtney was shaking. "How did we get here?"

"Don't know," D.L. said, squeezing her tighter. "But who cares? This is sweet. I haven't surfed in forever. I hope we never go back. This sure beats detention."

I tried not to look at him. Why wasn't he panicked like Courtney? Or me? He was probably in shock. Because teleporting to some random location—even a tropical one—was definitely something to freak out about. "Maybe we should get to shore?" I suggested before he started flipping out, too. I lay down on the surfboard and started paddling my arms just like they do it on TV.

By the time we made it to the beach, I was completely out of breath. Surfing was pretty exhausting.

But Courtney had a burst of energy. She ran all the way to a little juice bar farther up the beach. D.L. chased after her. And seeing as I couldn't lose them if I ever wanted to return them to Goode, I mustered up the strength to stand up and go after them.

"Wait up," I called out.

Big surprise. They both ignored me.

When I finally caught up, D.L. was trying to pull Courtney away from the counter. The guy working there was looking at her like she escaped the nut house. Courtney fought to get loose from D.L.'s hold. "You don't understand," she told the counter guy. "We were in the middle of detention in Pennsylvania and then ended up here."

"Dude, your girlfriend's losing it," the guy told D.L.

"I am not *losing* it," she said, swinging around at turbo speed. It caught D.L. off balance causing him to lose his footing and knock his head on the counter. He was out cold. But still breathing.

"I'll see if there's a doctor around here," the counter guy said, running out onto the beach.

"Oh my God. Oh my God. Oh my God. Oh my

God. Did I just kill him? D.L., please wake up." She hunched over him and lifted his head. "Please."

"He's going to be okay," I said.

A tear slid down her cheek as she looked at him. "He has to be. We have to get out of here. We've got to get him home."

I wasn't used to seeing this side of Courtney. The side where she thought about someone other than herself. I guess she was way into D.L.

"Just calm down," I told her. "Everything will be okay." She seemed so helpless. Even though I can't stand her, I felt the need to reassure her.

"No, it won't. We don't even know how we got here."

"This is all a dream." I had to tell her something.

"If this was a dream, *you* would not be here."

My sympathy for her was waning. Even in panic mode, Courtney was evil. "Fine. You're having a nightmare."

A local checked out D.L., while Courtney stood hovering over him. The doctor told us he'd be fine and would come to shortly—to just let him rest a little. Then he excused himself to get back to his luau.

"You're having a luau?" I asked. "I always wanted to go to one of those."

"Join us," he said. "Both of you."

"I'm not leaving D.L.," Courtney declared.

She was right. We needed to stay with him, and I needed to get us home. Although, Gabi would totally give me a hard time when I got back. She would say I should have at least tried to have a little fun while I was here. That I needed to lighten up. Maybe she was right. I was always taking things too seriously. "Let's wake D.L. up," I suggested. "Then we can all go to the luau."

"No," the doctor said. "The boy needs his rest. Let him come to on his own."

The guy behind the stand offered to watch him for us, so we could go to the luau. I wasn't so sure about leaving him there, but when a woman sitting nearby with her two little kids promised she'd keep her eye on him, too, I felt reassured.

"Cool, let's go," I said, figuring the more fun Courtney had, the more likely she'd believe the whole thing was a dream. I mean, really, how often did you get to go to a luau on a random Tuesday when you were supposed to be in school?

"We are not going with a stranger," Courtney protested.

Normally, I would have agreed with her. But the

luau was going on about twenty feet away, and we were stuck there until D.L. came to, anyway. What else was there to do? Just stare at him sleeping? Besides the guy at the counter said a local DJ was hosting the luau and broadcasting it live on his show. Sounded safe to me. If anything went wrong, I would just scream for help. Not only would everyone around hear me, but all his listeners would, too.

"Well, you can stay," I told Courtney, "but I'm going." I deserved a little fun. My life had been pretty awful lately. And this was Hawaii! I was going to make Gabi proud.

Courtney looked at D.L. laying there unconscious. "You're not leaving me here alone." She sneered at me. "I can't believe I'm going to a party with *you*."

"It's your dream," I said. "You picked me to be here, not the other way around. I guess deep down you must wish we still hung out." Okay, I couldn't resist messing with her just a little.

She didn't answer, just followed me over to the crowd.

"Welcome," a woman said, putting flowered leis around our neck. They smelled so good. They were real flowers, not the fake plastic ones I pictured us getting for the dance.

I didn't know what to take in first. The water was gorgeous. The color was almost turquoise. Not like the lake in Goode which was a mix of brown and green and only the brave dared go in.

Everything in Hawaii was beautiful, and the people at the party were nice. Nothing like the people I went to school with. They even told us to help ourselves to the food. There were colorful drinks and a whole buffet out there, including a giant roasted pig with an apple in its mouth. (I tried not to look at it, though. I don't like to eat—or even see—food that still has its head attached.)

What really caught my attention, though, was a group of three women hula dancing over to the side. They were wearing grass skirts and moving their hips better than Shakira. I waited until they finished a number, took Courtney by the wrist, and went up to the woman in the middle. She seemed the nicest—warm eyes. "Can you show us how to do that?"

She agreed and pretty soon I was shaking my hips like I'd been hula dancing my whole life. It was super fun. Even Courtney couldn't help but move to the music. I wanted to keep going, but I caught a glimpse of my watch. We had been there awhile. It was only a matter of time before Miss Simmons went back to class and noticed we were missing.

"We should go check on D.L.," I told Courtney.

She seemed to be over her fear and having a blast, because I practically had to drag her back to the juice stand to see how *her* boyfriend was doing.

D.L. still hadn't come to, but there was no time to waste. I was going to have to bring him back to school unconscious.

I grabbed one of D.L.'s hands and one of Courtney's. She looked at me funny with one eyebrow raised in the air. "Your dream," I said. Then I closed my eyes and chanted, "Bring us back to Goode. Bring us back to Goode." Courtney even joined in. But when I reopened my eyes, we weren't in the gloomy, detention classroom; we were still in sunny, fabulous Hawaii.

chapter
✦ 29 ✦

What was I going to do? We needed to get back
to school. ASAP. But without my powers working,
that was impossible. It wasn't like I could just go buy
three airline tickets.

There was no other option. My powers had to
function properly. I had to get us back before Miss
Simmons found us missing and contacted our parents.
My mother would no doubt call the police, the
local news, and even the Boy Scouts to form a search
party. That was not the kind of publicity I needed.

I want to go back! I want to go back! I thought
it, I said it, I even jumped up and down for emphasis.
Then I felt the ground give way. Was I teleporting us?
I looked down. Yep. I certainly was. Only not where
I had hoped. I managed to send us back in the water
on surfboards.

Courtney was struggling to keep D.L.'s head from going underwater. "I'm ready to wake up," she shrieked. I jumped onto her surfboard to help keep D.L. afloat. He was dead weight. And while I thought he was a complete jerk, I didn't want to see him die.

D.L. was really heavy. I didn't know how much longer we'd be able to manage with him. The water was coming up all around us. It even destroyed the leis around our necks. "Take us to school, please," I yelled as I watched the last of the flowers float away.

And my wish was granted. The three of us were standing at the front of a classroom. Too bad it wasn't *our* classroom. In fact, it wasn't even our school. I had gotten it wrong. Now twenty sets of eyes I had never seen before were glued on us.

"Sorry, wrong room," I said, as the class started erupting into chaos. The students looked like they were kindergarteners, and they were completely baffled by our unusual entrance. One girl started crying, which made the kid next to her break down in tears, too.

I was a little afraid Courtney would join in the cry fest, too.

"Wacky dream," I told her. "Keeps getting crazier."

A couple of screams filled the classroom and some

giggles. Finally, one little girl came up and grabbed onto my sleeve. "Aloha," she said.

We were still in Hawaii. The teacher shooed the child back to her seat.

"Who are you?" the teacher demanded of us. "How did you get here?"

"Ooh, ooh, I know," a boy in the second row called out, waving his hand in the air. "It was magic."

"Ha!" I said, trying to humor him. "We came through the door. You saw that, right?" I hoped I could get at least one of the kids to agree with me. "But this is the wrong room. We're going to get going now," I said, trying to drag D.L. to the door. "Sorry for the inconvenience." I couldn't move him on my own, so I forced Courtney to help me. She seemed in a trance, but listened to what I said. "Hurry up," I told her.

I was definitely getting my exercise in for the day. Possibly the whole week. We dropped D.L. outside the door and sat next to him, our backs to the wall. I just needed to catch my breath, but I could hear the teacher paging someone on the intercom. There was no time to rest.

"We want to be back in Miss Simmons's classroom in Goode, Pennsylvania," I said adding extra detail this time as a precaution. I didn't want to land in some classroom she taught in years ago. "Send us there!"

It wasn't working. And I could hear footsteps getting closer. We were going to get in tons of trouble if anyone caught us.

My heart sped up and my breath felt frozen inside of me. "Now!" I managed to get out.

Then it happened. We were back in Miss Simmons's classroom, just like we never left. Something finally went right.

chapter
✦30✦

Courtney was up in my face, like before my powers went out of control, and D.L. was seated in his desk. Had I brought us back to the very moment before my powers transported us?! How awesome would that be? Nothing to explain, no messes to clean up.

As I let out a sigh of relief, I got another look at D.L. He wasn't just seated at his desk; he was slumped over it. That meant he was still unconscious. And he was soaking wet. I hadn't undone anything.

"Thank God," Courtney said, taking a step back to inspect her surroundings. She ran over to D.L. and shook him. He finally came to.

"What's going on?" he asked, rubbing the back of his head.

Courtney's face scrunched up like a shar-pei's. "Wait. Am I still dreaming?"

"Forget what just happened. Forget what just happened. Forget what just happened," I whispered as Courtney stared at her boyfriend.

D.L. gave her a super big, cocky grin. "You dream about me?"

Barf. Gross. Did I really need to be a part of this? "You're awake now," I answered before I was forced to listen to them profess their undying love for each other. But at least D.L. wasn't talking about surfing or Hawaii. Did that mean my chant worked?

"I don't remember waking up," Courtney complained. "So either I'm still dreaming or everything that just happened was real."

I took a seat and pulled out my copy of *Romeo and Juliet*. "Forget what just happened," I whispered again.

I crossed my fingers that it would do the trick. "What is going on?" Courtney complained. "How did we get back here?"

Shoot. She still remembered, but at least D.L. was looking at her like she was talking Pig Latin. Maybe I managed to make him forget.

"You're awake, but you were sleeping before. I saw you," I said and pretended to study the pages of the play. But really I was keeping my eyes on Courtney.

If she could jog D.L.'s memory, it would be only a millisecond before they linked everything back to me, and my secret became public knowledge.

Courtney wasn't buying my lies. "I'd remember getting up. I *don't* fall asleep in school." She turned her attention to D.L. "You remember, don't you? The water, surfing, Hawaii, whacking your head, right?"

"Barely remember walking into detention. Everything is kind of a blur," he said, with a shrug of his shoulder.

Major relief. I don't know if it was my powers or D.L.'s injury that made him forget. But I was certainly happy that he couldn't recall what happened.

"You've got to remember." Courtney was almost pleading with him. "I'm not making this up. We ended up in Hawaii, you almost drowned, then we poofed into some random class and now we're back."

D.L. watched her like she was putting on some out there one-woman show.

"Weird dream," I offered.

"It was not a dream," she yelled, walking over to me. "You were there, too. We went to a party."

"You two at a party together?" D.L. asked, leaning back in his chair. "Must have been a dream. That would never happen."

"It did," she protested. Then her eyebrows got high. "Your head," she said to D.L. "You were rubbing it. Explain that."

"It hurt."

"Exactly," she cried out. "Because you bumped it on the counter in Hawaii."

"No, he didn't." I had to stop this before it shook D.L.'s memory. "Umm, he hit it on the back of the chair when he fell asleep. I guess it's just that this room is so warm. You both conked out. It was funny. I wish I took a picture."

"Then why are we all wet? Huh? Explain that!"

Ooh. That was going to be a lot tougher. "The sprinklers went off."

"That makes no sense. Then everything would be wet. But it's not. It's only us. I know you're behind this somehow," she told me. "You were chanting all this random stuff. Maybe you made everything happen."

She needed to be stopped from this line of thought. But how?

I looked around the science room. There was only one way. To fess up. "You're right. It was me."

"Knew it," Courtney yelled.

"I dumped the water." Come on, it wasn't like I

was really going to admit the truth. "You wanted an underwater theme for the dance so bad, so I decided to let you have one. I filled the garbage can with water from the sink and poured it on you."

"Then why are you wet, too?" Courtney asked, flashing between disbelief and pure anger.

"The can was so heavy I had trouble controlling it. So the water got on me, too . . ."

"I don't believe you," Courtney declared. "I know what I saw. We were in Hawaii."

"Maybe you were just dreaming about being there because of the water. Ever think of that?"

She sunk into the chair closest to her. "We were there."

"Court, it does sound pretty out there," D.L. said.

"Really," I said, using the opening D.L. gave me. "People are going to think you're nuts. What sounds more reasonable? Me dumping water on you or me teleporting you to Hawaii?" I laughed for effect. "But go ahead, tell everyone you went surfing during detention. I can't wait to hear what they say about you."

She sneered at me, and put her head in her hands. She knew I was right. "But I saw it. You, me, it was all—" She squeezed her forehead.

I got up and moved next to her. "Believe me, if I

had the power to send people on exotic vacations, you would definitely *not* be on my list. Unless it was sending you somewhere far, far away from me."

"There was hula dancing and a classroom and a giant wave . . ." Courtney's voice sounded meek. "And D.L. hit his head and almost drowned."

He reached out and touched her arm. "Cor, I'm pretty sure I'd remember something like that."

That's what he thought.

"Fine," Courtney said, looking up at me. "Maybe you did dump the water." She didn't sound convinced, but she was going along with it, anyway. "Then I'm sure Cole's going to love hearing all about this one."

I cringed. Once again my powers were going to result in me seeming like a horrible person to the guy I adored. I couldn't take it. When were things going to go my way? Wasn't it time for my powers to start working for me, not against me? But that didn't seem like it would ever happen. And I was sick of it. It was time for a change. If I couldn't make my powers work to my advantage, I knew someone who could. Angel Garrett's luck was about to change.

chapter

31

One good thing came out of my trip to Hawaii—
two, if you count that I got a mini-vacation—and that
was: I could now stop the pencil midair. Compared
to the wave, Lou's lesson was amateurish. Besides, I
had better use for that pencil. I was using it to make
a list. On why it was a good idea to have my father
use his skills to make Cole ask me to the dance and
dump Jaydin:

1. It was just asking, and once we got there, Cole
   would remember how much he likes me.
2. I'd be saving Cole from going with Jaydin, who
   was sneaky and awful, even if he couldn't tell.
3. Powers got me into this mess with Cole,
   powers should get me out.
4. Cole's supercute, and I miss him giving me that
   big, lopsided grin.

5. The dance would stink if I didn't have a date.

6. Cole and I belonged together.

Of course there were the cons, too . . .

1. Powers always mess things up.

2. People should be able to make up their own minds without evil influences.

The pros totally outweighed the cons, but the cons were pretty big ones. I was torn.

"Hello, there," Lou said, popping in from nowhere.

"Ever heard of calling first?" I crumpled up my list and put it under my pillow. There was no reason to let Lou in on my plan until I was sure that I was going to go through with it.

He bowed his head to me. "My apologies."

"It's okay," I said. Besides, I didn't want to be too hard on him. There was a good chance I'd be asking him for that Cole favor. "I'm ready for the next lesson," I said, and sent the pencil flying through the air, and then stopped it two feet out to prove my case.

"Great." He pulled out his hPhone to check on the next lesson and then put it back in his jacket pocket. "Now you need to make it return to you. I want you to have full control over which direction it moves, the speed, everything."

"Come on," I said, jumping off my bed. "I can do way more advanced stuff than that. I already—" I cut myself off. I didn't need him to know about my accidental trips. "I mean, I already mastered the moving it forward and stopping it. How hard can making a pencil go in a circle be? Can't you teach me something cool, like how to look into someone's soul, spy on them, make objects appear out of nowhere?"

He shook his head no. "You are not ready for that kind of thing. The basics will teach you control. There are a lot of different aspects to your gift. Don't underestimate having a good foundation. Each skill I'm showing you plays into a bigger whole. And just because you have a couple of the basics down doesn't mean the others will be so easy. If an artist begins working with clay on a Tuesday, do you think he'll be able to create a beautiful sculpture that same night?"

"Probably," I said.

Lou shook his head. "No. Not without going through a process. He has to get used to the clay, learn how to mold it, and so on. It takes time. Technique. He doesn't become a master overnight."

"Fine," I said. I wasn't looking for a lecture.

"Don't look so sad," he said. "You know if you need to do something advanced, just ask. I'd be happy to make it happen."

"Thanks," I moved in and gave him a big hug. "I really appreciate you teaching me."

Lou looked genuinely surprised. I wasn't in the habit of giving him hugs. The truth was, today was no exception.

I wasn't embracing my father, I was pickpocketing him.

chapter
✦ 32 ✦

Evil, crazy, or stupid? I definitely possessed at least one of those personality traits. How else did I wind up stealing from the devil?

But that's what I did. Right as I was giving him a big ol' bear hug, I reached into his jacket pocket and scooped up his hPhone. While I do not condone stealing, this was life or death. Well, life or death for my relationship with Cole. Before I continued with my plans to get him back, I had to know a few things. Like, did Courtney poison him against me completely? Did he ask Jaydin out because he liked her or because she just happened to be there? Did he have any feelings left for me at all? These were things that could only be found out by spying.

Sure, Lou said he'd help me out. But really? Did I want my *father* knowing all the minute details of my love life? I think not. So I went the juvenile delinquent route.

Once Lou was gone, I pulled out the hPhone. The plan seemed a lot more ingenious before I had the device in my possession. It had a lot of icons. How was I supposed to know what to do? I wasn't very familiar with it. Lou had shown me a thing or two, but at the moment that didn't seem like much. I hunted down the icon with the halo on it and pushed it. Lou had told me that was the application for everything involving me. After scrolling down a bit, I saw Cole's name. I took a deep breath and clicked again.

The screen changed, and I was looking right into Cole's house. He was sitting around the dining room table with his parents. The screen was tiny, so I hit zoom and the picture was immediately projected onto my wall.

I could see everything, the scuff marks near the bottom of the light peach walls, the gray in his dad's goatee, the dachshund waiting under the table for them to drop food, Cole's dad reaching down and slipping the dog some chicken when Mrs. Daniels turned away. It all looked so real, like I was really there.

They talked about lots of things—their days, the news—but my name never came up. But I could be patient. I could wait. Besides, I always said I could watch Cole all day. The only thing missing was the popcorn. I reached into my top drawer and pulled out some goodies. I keep a stash there so whenever my mom sends me to my room I have something to keep me entertained. No popcorn, but there was a bag of Tootsie Rolls.

My mouth salivated a little when Cole's mom brought out dessert. An incredibly gooey-looking chocolate cake. Sure beat my candy. Cole downed his in three seconds flat and went in for a second piece.

"That's your sister's mud cake," his mother said, slapping away his hand. "For when she gets back from dance practice."

"Becca's not here. She loses," he protested, reaching for it again. "She doesn't like it that much, anyway. It's my favorite."

Mrs. Daniels pulled the cake away right as Cole was about to stab it with his fork.

He opened his mouth to complain, but just as he was about to speak, his phone rang.

"Hey, Jaydin," Cole said, answering it. He looked at his mother and then back down. Then his voice got super low. "Yeah," he said. Then he uttered something else, but it was impossible to make out.

He was a really good whisperer. He must not have wanted his mom to hear, but it was making it hard for me to hear, too! "Yeah," he said again.

I was getting absolutely nothing from this conversation. What was Jaydin saying? I needed to eavesdrop on her side of the conversation, too. What if she was telling him about what I did in detention? I'm sure Courtney filled her in on everything. Or worse, what if they were talking about the dance? Or how much he loved her?

There had to be an icon on the hPhone to let me raise the audio or split screens so I could be in both of their houses at once.

"Sure," Cole said into the phone, his mouth curling up into that grin I loved.

What was he sure-ing? This conversation couldn't have been going on without me. I tapped on a few icons. Then some other ones. I *had* to know what those two were saying. But nothing was happening. I was tapping on two, three icons at a time, when suddenly there was a flash of light, and I was pulled up off my feet and sucked into the phone. Then, just like a spitball from a straw, I was shot out. Right into Cole's living room.

chapter
33

This was bad. Very bad. Cole and his family were no more than ten feet away from me. I ducked down behind the couch. The fireworks and the tree were nothing compared to this. I had to get out of there. If Cole or his family caught me, I'd look even more like an obsessed crazy person, which I suppose I was in a way . . . but I didn't mean to break into his house!

How did I get out of there? I pulled out the phone and hit the Angel icon again. Nothing. Same when I hit Cole's name. What was I going to do? I thought about making a run for the front door, but there was no way to get to it without them noticing me. I would have given anything to be able to transport myself back to Hawaii at that very moment. Or outer space.

My whole body stiffened as a light chiming sound approached. Moving my head slowly, I was able to see what it was. Cole's dog, his tags clinking together with each move. He stopped right in front of me and cocked his head to the side. I put my fingers to my lips. It had no effect on the dog. He started barking like crazy.

"What's wrong, Sammy?" Mrs. Daniels asked, her voice coming closer.

No. No. NO. I slid and shimmied my whole body under the couch. For once, being as flat as a board came in handy. I was able to fit. Barely.

The dog kept yapping. *Please, Sammy! Stop*, I thought. *I'll buy you all the bones you could ever want*. But he wouldn't let up.

"Something under there? Cole, will you take a look for me? I can't bend."

"Jaydin, I have to call you back." He sounded disappointed to hang up, which would have totally bummed me out if I wasn't in panic mode. "What's up, Sam?" he asked. "What did you find?"

Cole was about to see me stuffed under his couch. Life can be cruel. I closed my eyes, squished my arms to my side, making myself as small as I could, and prepared for Cole's scream of fear and disgust when he discovered me hiding in his house.

As I did, my hands hit something in my pocket. I

felt around. Yes. The tootsie rolls. I opened one up and pushed it over to Sam.

He grabbed it greedily and ran to the other side of the living room.

"Whoa, what do you have there?" I could hear Cole go after his dog. They seemed to be struggling. "I can't get it away from him."

Mr. Daniels joined the rest of the family to try and wrestle the tootsie roll away from Sam. I used that as a chance to move. I slithered out the back of the couch and crawled under the dining room table. At least there I could have my hands free to maneuver the hPhone.

"Chocolate is not good for dogs," Mrs. Daniels lectured Cole. I could hear Sam bark as they pried the treat from his teeth.

"It wasn't me," he objected. "Talk to Becca."

I didn't want to get him in trouble or make his dog sick, but I was desperate. The hPhone was my only hope. I hit icons. Every icon. Any icon.

"Hell-o," a voice on the other end said. I tried to hang up, but it wasn't working. The whole phone was flashing. I had pushed so many icons; they must have been interfering with one another. "How can I help you?" the voice continued. I covered the speaker with my hand to hush it.

"What is that?" Mrs. Daniels asked.

Not again. They were going to get me. In a last ditch effort, I threw a tootsie roll into the kitchen to draw their attention away from me and crawled toward the front door. I just needed to make it to the safety of the front lawn.

As I approached the door, it swung open pushing me behind it.

"Hey," a voice called out.

"It's just Becca," Cole said.

Phew. His sister came to my rescue. Not only did they think it was she who had been talking, but I was now safely hidden behind the door.

"*Just* Becca," she said, as she made her way into the living room. "Nice."

"Do we live in a barn?" Mrs. Daniels asked her. "Go shut the door."

I prayed she was a bratty daughter who would disobey her mother, but the hand reaching around the door told me that wasn't the case.

Well, my time in Goode was nice. I wondered where the juvenile detention board would send me once the Daniels pressed charges. Probably some school for problem children. I clutched my hand around the hPhone. Why had I been so stupid? I wished I never turned the thing on. Then I realized I hadn't tried one thing. Shutting it off. With a quick push, I did it. The phone was off, and I was sucked back in—and right back to my bedroom.

That was it. I had figured it out. I got myself back before I got caught. "Thank God," I said.

"Not quite." Lou was hovering over me, his light eyes now black. He held out his hand. "You have something of mine, I believe." His voice was crisp.

I put the phone in his hand, but refused to look at him. I had never seen Lou this angry. It was scary.

"You're stealing from me?"

I thought silence was the best response. Apparently he didn't think so. "Well? I'm waiting for an answer."

"Sorry," I mumbled. "But shouldn't you be proud?" I questioned. "I'm taking after you." I flashed him a smile, making sure my dimples popped out. It was one of the physical traits we shared. I hoped seeing them would remind him that I was his daughter and not some misfit for him to banish to the underworld.

"No," he said, his voice firm. "I have higher hopes for you."

I thought punishment from my mother was bad,

but I had a hunch it was like a slice of mud cake in comparison to what the devil could dole out.

"Are you going to make me shovel coal for the rest of eternity?" I asked, clutching onto my comforter. It was possibly the last soft, comfortable thing I'd ever touch.

"What?" he asked, his eyes slightly lightening.

"Isn't that what you do? Send people down below and make them shovel coal into the flames of Hades?"

He laughed. "You watch way too many horror movies." He put his hand on my shoulder. "Angel, you're my daughter. I am not going to take your soul for disobeying me. But I'm not happy, and you will be punished if you do it again."

"Do it again? Does that mean I'm off the hook?"

"This time," he said, giving me an I-mean-business look.

"And you're not going to tell Mom, right? I don't want her to know about my powers. Not yet."

He shook his head. "I still think that's a mistake. But if that's what you want, I won't tell her, as long as you stay out of trouble."

"Thank you," I said, wrapping my arms around him. This time the hug was real, but he checked his pockets, anyway.

"Now what were you trying to do with this?" he asked, patting the phone. "I told you I'd help you if you needed something. What do you need?"

"Nothing," I said. I had seen more than enough. Cole was no longer into me. It was one thing to go after his forgiveness. But getting him to choose me over Jaydin was completely different. Jaydin was beautiful and popular. How could I possibly compete with that?

chapter

34

"Look at her," I said to Gabi, "trying to tempt Cole with her muffins. Big deal. So she can bake. I could probably bake, too, if I tried." I couldn't take my eyes off the doorway to homeroom. That's where Cole was standing with Jaydin. She had just handed him the muffin when I walked in. I heard her say she made it herself. "How can he like her?" I felt my fists clench as Jaydin tossed her head back and laughed at something Cole said.

"Beats me. But you'll win him back," Gabi said.

"No, I won't," I said, pounding my fist onto my desk. "The dance is almost here. He's not going to cancel on *her*. He's had it with me."

"You can't give up," Gabi said, shifting her whole body to face me. "You have to up your game. Don't let one of Courtney's groupies win."

"I don't know . . ."

"Well, I do." She leaned closer to me. "She might be able to make muffins, but can she send him to outer space? Just think about everything you can do."

My eyes followed Cole as he took his seat. Gabi was right. I needed to fight harder. I couldn't give up on him. He was too cute. Watching him toss a piece of the muffin into his mouth made me angry. Cole wasn't Jaydin's. He was mine. I could totally top a muffin. I had powers.

I leaned down to make it look like I was getting something out of my bag. But what I was really doing was conjuring up a fabulous piece of mud cake. Sure, Lou said he'd punish me if he found out I did something advanced—something he didn't teach me. But really, how advanced was making a cake? Gabi was churning them out in her Easy-Bake Oven at five years old. This was nothing.

I molded the air with my hands, concentrated, and, for once, my powers actually did what I wanted.

Right in my hands, sitting perfectly on a plate was a duplicate of the cake I saw in Cole's house last night. His favorite dessert. *Take that, Jaydin.*

When he was seated, I tapped Cole on the shoulder. He turned around and his eyes instantly went to the cake. My plan was already working.

"Do you want this?" I asked, offering up the plate, fork included. "I already had a big piece for breakfast and can't eat any more."

"Sure," Cole said, his eyes totally huge. He didn't even put up a fuss. I guess when it came to cake he was able to forgive me no problem.

A little bit of frosting got on my finger as I handed it to him. Once he turned around, I licked it off. But the taste was not exactly what I had envisioned. It was mud cake, all right.

MADE WITH REAL MUD.

There was no sugar or chocolate, just wet dirt. I spit it out, and wiped my tongue with my hand. The taste was disgusting. Then I got that all too familiar feeling in the pit of my stomach—the one that felt like a dozen Smurfs having a tug-of-war with my intestines. Because I had done it again. I made an already bad situation with Cole worse. I had to get the cake away from him before he tried it. He would think it was an evil practical joke if I let him dig into a plate of mud.

"Cole, wait," I said, while frantically getting out of my chair and moving toward the cake.

He was about to put the fork to his lips. "Don't," I shouted, knocking it from his hand and grabbing the plate.

"What's your problem?" he asked.

"I saw a hair in it," I said. "You can't eat it."

"If you didn't want to give me the cake, you shouldn't have."

"That's not it," I protested. "I really saw a hair."

"Right." He picked up his pen and began to doodle on his math homework. All of his focus was on it. He wouldn't look up, not even when I said his name.

Cole didn't believe me. He thought I was trying to mess with him. I took my seat. Why couldn't anything ever go right?

chapter

35

"Now we definitely need a spotlight dance for the king and queen," Courtney said, going on and on about the dance during detention. She was positive she was going to be crowned, and I was pretty sure she was right.

The dance was going to have Gabi's Hollywood theme. Courtney decided that after her "dream" the other day, she didn't want anything to do with underwater or Hawaii. I had to agree.

"I got the yearbook club to agree to take pictures of us on the red carpet. I want everyone to get really dressed up. Just like an awards ceremony. My mom picked up silver foil paper to make the stars for the walls. We can cut them here, and I'm making my study hall help out, too. I want to see a ton of helium balloons filling the ceiling. But they can't be a bunch of colors. We need to stick with silver, white, and black. Elegant stuff. Miss Simmons is going to watch over the king and queen voting to make sure there's no cheating." Courtney smirked at me. "Unless of course you want to do that, Angel. Since you don't have anyone to dance with."

"Thanks, I'll pass," I answered, refusing to let her draw me into a fight.

"That's probably for the best," she said. "I wouldn't trust you, anyway." After getting in her jab at me, she went right back to coordinating the dance. "So what about snacks? What should we have?"

I tuned her out. She could plan whatever she wanted. I didn't care. There was no way I was ever setting foot in there.

chapter 36

Cole made it pretty clear he no longer liked me. Eight whole days went by and he didn't talk to me once. Not once! And I really tried to get him to. But he refused to utter a sound or, worse, even acknowledge me. Not when I stood behind him in line in the cafeteria and asked him which looked more edible—the hamburger or the lasagna, or when I accidentally-on-purpose dropped my pencil under his desk and asked him to get it for me (I even tapped him on the shoulder hard and still got no answer), or even when I blocked his entrance to homeroom. He just waited for me to move. It was official. I no longer existed in Cole Daniels's universe.

And the dance was the next day.

I couldn't stop watching Cole's table during lunch. Everyone seemed so excited. Courtney, Jaydin, and

Lana were all smiles. Even Cole, D.L., Reid, and all their guy friends looked happy. It had to be the dance that was making them all so giddy.

My table, on the other hand, was doom and gloom central. Not even chocolate chip cookies and Twix bars could cheer me up. Seeing Cole give Jaydin that lopsided grin of his (that should have been saved for me) ruined my appetite. Even for sweets.

"Hey," Gabi said. "Are you listening to me?"

"Sorry." The only thing on my mind was Cole. And Cole and Jaydin. And Cole at the dance. Without me. Basically, all Cole, all the time.

"Cheer up," she said, picking at her tofu bologna. "After tomorrow night, it's all over."

That wasn't true. It was just starting. Cole and Jaydin were making their debut for the whole world to see. After that, everyone would link them together. The whole school would be talking about the dance and how Caydin was the new supercouple. (That even sounded better than Cangel—which just made me think of cankles—big, fat ankles.) I'd have to watch them walking hand in hand in the hallways. Maybe even see them steal a kiss during lunch. They'd probably get a page devoted to them in the yearbook. Then it would be there for me to see forever—in black and white.

"I gotta go," I said to Gabi. She didn't need to see me cry. No one did.

As I rushed toward the exit, I collided right into Cole at the garbage can. "I'm sorry," I said, looking up at him. "For everything."

Then I ran. As fast as I could.

chapter
✦ 37 ✦

"Good news," Miss Simmons told us. "I'm not going to make you serve detention tomorrow since it's so close to the dance start time. Today is your last day."

We all let out sighs of relief.

"But you do have to get to the gymnasium early tomorrow night to help set up for the dance," she said.

"I'm not going," I said. There was no way I was going to subject myself to watching Cole on a date with someone else.

"You have to," she answered. "It's part of being on the committee."

I started to protest, but she gave me a stern look and left for the teachers' room.

Courtney gloated. "No date, Angel? Big surprise there. Just go with your loser friend." She glared at Gabi. "Or there's always Max."

"Ignore her," Gabi said.

But that was hard.

"Think about something else," Gabi whispered. "We don't need your powers going all crazy." I wasn't too worried. I had been practicing my lessons at home. While I hadn't mastered the latest one, the first two were simple. Powers weren't my problem. The dance was.

"What are you going to wear?" Gabi asked.

"Huh?"

"To the dance."

"Who cares?" I said. It wasn't like I had anyone to impress anymore. Besides, I was just going to hang up the decorations and leave. Before Caydin showed up.

"Well, I think I'm going to wear the dress I wore to my cousin Josh's bar mitzvah. It's dark blue . . ."

I put my head down on my desk as she rattled on about her outfit. But none of that mattered. The only thing on my mind was how to survive middle school without Cole.

Step one: making it through the dance.

chapter
38

Gabi looked like she stepped off the page of some teen magazine's prom issue. "Your dress is so fancy," I said, eyeing her dark blue gown. It had an empire waist with a ribbon cutting right underneath her chest, the dress hung to the floor and tied around her neck. "What happened to wearing what you wore to your cousin's bar mitzvah?"

"This is what I wore," she said, yanking at her French braid. "I described the dress to you yesterday. If you had bothered listening, you'd know."

I looked at her dress and then at my jumper. It was like a *Teen Vogue* meets *Romper Room* smackdown. Don't get me wrong, my outfit was way cute—black jumper, tights, and a white blouse. It was the one I wore on my first date with Cole. I looked fine, but Gabi looked like she was going to the Oscars. Which I guess was the point.

Not that any of it mattered. Jeans and a T-shirt would have been good enough. I only even put the jumper on because I wanted Miss Simmons to think I was taking my dance committee responsibilities seriously. Otherwise she'd probably give me another week of detention. But I was just there to hang decorations and leave—before Cole and Jaydin showed up.

"We should go in," Gabi said.

"Wait," I said, putting out my arm to stop her. We were standing at the side of the school, and I could hear Courtney approaching the front entrance. (I'd know her annoying squeal anywhere.) There was no reason to suffer through any more time with her than necessary, so I was going to wait. I carefully peeked my head around the corner to sneak a look at what she was wearing. "NO," I said in a harsh whisper.

Not only was it Courtney and D.L., but *Cole* and *Jaydin*. They weren't supposed to be there to set up. They weren't on the committee. I wanted to spare myself the pain of seeing them on their date. What could be more horrendous? And to make matters worse, they both looked so good.

Jaydin had on a shift dress that my mother never would have let me wear. It was silvery and crazy short.

She had her black hair piled on top of her head in a messy bun and she was even wearing makeup. Black eyeliner that she smudged all around her eyes for a smoky look. She looked at least sixteen. Cole was probably thinking he went temporarily insane for ever wanting to hang out with me instead of her. Even though I didn't want to admit it, she looked amazing.

Not as amazing as Cole, though. He was wearing a suit. I had never seen him in one before. He looked so cute. His tie was blue with silver stripes. Probably to match Jaydin's dress. Gross. I didn't want to think about that anymore, so my eyes drifted to D.L. He was in a suit, too, and looking pretty good for an absolute jerk. Courtney had her arm linked through his. She was in some black-and-white fitted gown that looked like she stole it straight from the set of *Gossip Girl*. Her hair was in a side bun, without a bit of frizz to be found anywhere. The dress even brought out her tan which was probably thanks to me and the little Hawaiian field trip I sent her on.

"I can't go in," I told Gabi.

"You have to," she said, peering over at Courtney and company as they walked into the school. "It's part of detention. You don't want to get in more trouble."

I wasn't so sure about that. More trouble seemed

like a good alternative to watching Cole and Jaydin dance together.

Gabi grabbed my arm. "Let's get it over with."

"Fine," I conceded. "But not like this. I need a new dress."

"We don't have time for you to go get changed."

"Good thing we don't have to go anywhere," I said. "I'm going to whip something up right here."

"How did I know you were going to say that? Angel," she said putting her hands in a steeple and pleading with me, "you know something's going to go wrong. Don't do it. Lou will find out, and you'll get in big trouble."

That made me pause for a second. Lou warned me that if I used my powers when I wasn't supposed to, not only would he punish me, but he'd let my mom in on my secret. But Lou wasn't chaperoning the dance, and he promised he wouldn't spy on me—so there really wasn't anything to worry about. I was in the clear. "He's not going to find out."

"Okay, then remember what happened last time you tried to change your outfit? You ended up half-naked."

"That's why I'm going to make sure to word my command very carefully," I assured her. Gabi shook her head at me. I chose to ignore her. Obviously I knew there was a certain amount of risk when it came to using my "special gift." But there was also a risk in walking into the dance in the outfit I had on. Courtney and her friends would definitely make fun of me for being underdressed and for having worn the jumper before, and Cole would think I was a handmaiden in comparison to his princess date. How much worse could I make things?

"Keep lookout," I told Gabi, and held up my hand before she protested again. It was time to focus. I closed my eyes and envisioned the dress I wanted. Black, tight, and short. Something very Mara's Daughters. I waved my hands over my body, as if I was molding the dress. I opened one eye. Nothing had changed. Why couldn't I just wiggle my nose like that witch I saw on some Nick at Nite show? Why did my powers have to be so stubborn?

"I don't want to be a mess, so give me the perfect dress," I chanted as I continued to move my arms around.

"Oh my God," Gabi said. "It's working. It's changing."

She was right. My jumper started to morph. The sleeves disappeared, and the skirt and blouse melded together. It was working! I was going to have a killer dress.

But then the bottom started to pouf out. What was going on? I didn't want a pouf. I wanted to look sleek. A lace petticoat started to form underneath the dress, a bow started to form, and to top it off, the whole thing was a putrid orange. This was not what I wanted at all!

"Oooh, it's so cute," Gabi said.

"I don't want to be *cute*." The spit flew from my mouth as I uttered the word. I was going for sexy rocker, not the marshal of the Easter parade. This had to be fixed.

With my hands pushing against the bottom of the dress, I declared, "Take away the pouf."

"Careful," Gabi shouted out. "Remember—"

"Right. But with fabric, lots and lots of fabric. I don't want the dress to disappear."

The material started moving under my fingers, only it wasn't flattening. It was expanding down *and* out. I reached out to grab it, hoping to stop the fabric in its tracks. Only it wouldn't. It kept going. It was like having a gigantic bubble gum bubble wrapped around the bottom half of my body. From the corner of my eye, I could see two matching baby bubbles forming as sleeves.

"Nooooo," I cried. "Not *that* much fabric." I was wearing the ugliest dress in the history of ugly dresses. I was totally freaking out. "This is not what I wanted. I wanted something hot in black or gray or even red."

Gabi's eyes were like saucers. "You've got to calm down. The more worked up you get, the worse you make it."

"Not possible."

She looked down. "Umm."

"What?" I snapped.

She pointed to my butt. I looked over my shoulder, and wished the ground would swallow me up and send me straight to Hades. Or maybe I was already there, because right on my behind was a little design. Three lightening bolts. One in black. One in gray. And one in red. Mortifying. I didn't need people staring at my butt. "Lightening bolts weren't the kind of hot that I meant," I moaned. "And I wanted to change the dress to *one* of those colors!" I slapped my hands against my chest for emphasis. When I moved them away, there were two red handprints in their place.

"What am I going to do?" I asked, putting my hands on hips.

"First, relax," Gabi instructed. "You need to calm down before you try anything else."

That made sense. I shook my arms out.

"Uh-oh," Gabi said.

Following her gaze, my eyes dropped to my side. There were two more handprints where my hands had just been. "Enough," I shouted. "No more handprints." This was awful. I wanted something Cole would think was cool, not something that would send him into a laughing spasm.

I lightly touched the fabric on my stomach. It didn't leave a fingerprint. Nope, I had successfully stopped that. This time it left something else. A drawing of Cole's face appeared on my dress right over my belly.

"No. NO. NO. NO. ANYTHING but that," I yelled. The picture started changing, but it wasn't an improvement. It morphed to D.L.'s face. "No, I didn't mean anything. No people." On command, a big, fluorescent, yellow, smiley face appeared, covering the portrait.

Gabi had her hand over her mouth. She was probably trying to keep the "I told you so" from escaping her lips.

"Okay," I said, taking a deep breath. "I need to get this back to normal. No more crazy changes. I want—"

"What are you two doing over here," Miss Simmons said as she headed in our direction. "Get inside and help the others." I caught her eyeing my dress, as she got closer. "Um, that's an *interesting* dress, Angel. Very colorful."

That was to say the least. It was a putrid orange gown with a big bell bottom and poufy sleeves with red, gray, and black lightening bolts on my butt; red handprints above my chest and hips; and a big, fluorescent smiley face on my stomach. Interesting obviously translated into the most hideous thing she's ever laid eyes on.

And it was about to make its Goode Middle School debut in front of Courtney, Cole, and everyone else. Too bad the fashion police weren't real. I would have given anything to have been dragged away and put behind bars. It had to beat the firing squad I was about to face.

chapter
✦ 39 ✦

"No way," Jaydin shrieked, spotting me first, as I stepped into the gym. "You are not wearing that."

"Wow, Double-A," Courtney joined in. "Didn't think you could look worse than you normally do, but you managed to top it. Good job."

I'm pretty sure I saw Cole and D.L. do double takes, too, but I guess I couldn't really blame them. The dress looked like a kindergartener—a very untalented kindergartener—had designed it.

"Seriously," Jaydin said. "Did you misunderstand and think this was a circus theme?"

Courtney laughed. "She'd fit in well as the human freak show."

"Definitely," Jaydin agreed. "She kind of looks like one of those chimps they dress up in clothes. Only they're actually cute."

Gabi gripped my arm. "It's okay. Ignore them."

But I couldn't. "Aren't you all just hysterical? Ever think I'm making a statement that dressing up for some silly dance is pretentious and totally not necessary." Okay, that wasn't what I was trying to do, but it seemed better than saying I put on this monstrosity because I thought it actually looked good.

I grabbed some star cutouts and tape, turned away from them, and began slapping the decorations onto the wall. I was so tempted to teleport Courtney and company somewhere. Somewhere like the desert or to a lecture on the importance of astrophysics that goes on until eternity. Only I knew better. I wasn't going to do it. Lou would have my head. That is, if I even got them there.

"Whoa," D.L. said, laughing. "Trying to flash us all, Garrett?"

"Huh?"

He spoke like I couldn't understand English. "It was a joke," he said superslowly and sarcastically. "Because of the lightning *flashes* on your butt."

"Don't look at my butt," I yelled, covering it with my hands. "Don't you have decorations to hang up?" I stared him down until he got back to work. "This is torture," I whispered to Gabi.

She gave me a sympathetic look. At least Cole hadn't commented on my getup.

I worked crazy fast to hang as many decorations as I could. That way I could get out of there. After hanging my thirty-nine millionth star, I looked around the room. It actually looked pretty with all the silver cutouts on the wall, white helium balloons covering the ceiling, and red carpet leading from outside into the gym. The only thing that was downright gross-looking, other than my dress, of course, was the way Jaydin was up in Cole's face.

"Do you think this one should go here?" Jaydin asked him, holding a star. She was so close to him, their arms were touching.

I couldn't help myself. With a flick of my hand, I scooted her ten feet away.

"What the—" she cried out.

Gabi saw the smile creep up on my face, even though I was trying really hard to mask it. "What did you do?" she asked.

"Nothing," I said. Well, nothing other than practice my homework. Moving Jaydin across the room was just as easy as moving the pencil and one hundred times more fun.

Jaydin headed back toward Cole, but I stopped her in her tracks.

"Angel," Gabi said disapprovingly.

"What? Just lesson two." I was disappointed I hadn't figured out how to do lesson three, making the pencil go in every direction. It would have been great to send Jaydin zigzagging through the room. I thought about giving it a try and seeing if I could move her all around. But after my dress fiasco, I decided to listen to Lou's earlier warning about not using powers I hadn't mastered. Instead, I stuck with what I knew.

So when Jaydin took a step toward Cole, I sent her flying backward until she was up against the wall. They weren't going to get near each other. Not while I was watching. "What is happening?" she asked, clutching her head.

"Quit messing around," Courtney said. "People are going to be here any second, and I want everything perfect."

"I'm not doing it on purpose," she whined.

"Whatevs, Jaydin," Courtney said, waving her off. "You said you would help. Now stop fooling around and hang up the stars."

Jaydin opened up her mouth to protest, but shut it closed. There was no use talking back to Courtney.

"You okay?" Cole called out to her.

She nodded, rolled her eyes at Courtney, and made her way back toward Cole. Jaydin didn't deserve to be near someone like Cole. She was too nasty.

So when Cole turned his back to her to grab some decorations, I sent Jaydin back to the wall again. She looked completely baffled. But I had to give her credit. She was determined. No matter how many times I froze her in her tracks or sent her backward, she still tried to work her way back to Cole.

"You have to stop," Gabi said as I continued with my new favorite game. "People are starting to show up."

"So?" It wasn't like they could pin Jaydin's weirdness on me.

"So," Gabi repeated after me, "Cole is going to want to dance with his date. He's going to figure out she's not moving away on purpose. Do you really want to watch him chase *her* across the auditorium all night and try and figure out what's going on?"

Her words made me feel just as ugly as my dress. Cole wanted to be near Jaydin. Not me. And my power games were not going to change that.

chapter

40

"Come on," Gabi said. She guided me away from Cole and Jaydin and toward the ballot box for dance king and queen. A few people were already gathered around it.

"I'm definitely voting for Courtney," Brooke said. "And Cole."

"Court is going to kill you. She made it very clear we were supposed to vote for D.L.," Bronwyn reminded her. "She wants the spotlight dance with him."

"She'll never know. Besides, I like Cole better."

That made two of us.

"Well, I'm voting for D.L.," Bronwyn answered and tossed her ballot into the box.

Miss Simmons handed me my voting slips. "No thanks," I said. It was bad enough I was at the dance. I wasn't taking part in any of the stupid formalities involved with it.

"Come on," Miss Simmons nagged me. "You're part of the committee. Show some school spirit."

With a silent groan I took the slip. I quickly wrote down Gabi's name for queen and tossed it in the box. She didn't stand a chance at beating Courtney, but she was the only person I wanted to see get crowned. The vote for king was a lot harder. My gut said to pick Cole. I mean he was *my* king. But I couldn't bare the thought of him winning and dancing with Courtney. It was bad enough he was going to be with her best friend all night. So I wrote down D.L.'s name, even though it meant giving Courtney what she wanted. It was the lesser of the two evils.

"I've had enough," I told Gabi. "I'm outta here."

"You should try one more time with Cole," Gabi whispered. "Maybe there's still a chance. Apologize. For everything—ignoring him, being rude, standing him up. All of that."

"I don't know," I said, looking down at my nightmare of a dress. "It's probably too late for that. That may have worked a while ago, but it seems kind of hopeless now. He already thinks I'm a freak extraordinaire."

"Then what do you have to lose?"

The answer was *nothing*, so I decided to go for it. When I moved back to Cole, he was standing next to

Jaydin at the punch bowl. "Cole," I said, getting him to look in my direction while I sent Jaydin flying backward. "Can I talk to you for a sec?"

He didn't say anything, he just looked at me.

"I'm sorry for everything. I should never have ignored you or acted flaky. My life's just been crazy." I decided to go for the truth. Well, the semi-truth. "My dad came back into my life after being nonexistent for the past thirteen years. I guess it got me acting a little freaky." I bit at my nail and waited for him to answer.

"We should dance."

Only the words didn't come from him. They came from Jaydin. I hadn't been paying attention and she managed to sneak back up before I could stop her. Cole nodded at her.

I felt like one of the balloons in the room. One that had the helium sucked right out of it.

"Hey, Angel," Max said. "Cool dress."

Only Max could compliment a dress like the one I was wearing and sound like he actually meant it. "Thanks."

I could feel Jaydin watching us. No way was she going to the dance floor until she got all the juicy gossip she could.

"You think, maybe," Max said, kicking a plastic cup

that had fallen on the ground, "you'd want to dance with me?"

I heard Jaydin snort. And I wanted to cry. Was this what my life was going to be like? Destined to be with the nerd while someone else walked away with my king? My whole body felt numb.

"So . . ." Max asked, waiting for my answer.

I felt lower than low. I didn't want to dance. *Not with Max*. But, I said yes. At least I could do one good thing that night. Just because I was miserable didn't mean I had to mess up his evening, too. No one liked to get rejected. I knew that way too well.

"Cool," Max said, his whole face breaking into a smile. He leaned back, putting his hand on the table. He ended up knocking over a cup of juice.

"Watch it, you idiot," Jaydin spat. "You almost got my shoes."

Max dropped down and started wiping up the spill. "I'm sorry," he mumbled.

"No," I said. "You shouldn't be apologizing to her. She should apologize to you." Then I looked right at Jaydin. "Max is one of the nicest people in this stupid school. You don't even deserve to be in the same room as him. Let's go Max. She's making me sick."

I took his arm and pulled him toward the dance floor.

chapter

41

Max put his arms around my waist, and I forced myself not to let on how uncomfortable it made me. Even when I saw a drop of sweat roll down the side of his face.

"Thanks for dancing with me," Max said, temporarily moving his arm from around me to wipe his head. Then he put it right back. I'm sure there was a big sweat stain on my dress from where his arm was. Not that it mattered. Nothing could make this dress look any worse.

"Sure," I said, and prayed that he didn't stomp on my foot. It was like dancing with Frankenstein. He moved me round and round in stiff, jolting steps. Why couldn't it have been a fast song?

"This dance rocks," he said, turning me so I was looking right at Cole and Jaydin. She had her hands around his neck, while he had his on her hips. They were looking at each other intensely and talking about something. Probably how much they loved each other and were so happy to be hanging out together and other gag-worthy stuff.

"Yeah, it really rocks all right," I managed to answer, my voice a little shaky. How could Cole like someone like me and then go for someone like Jaydin? We were nothing alike. Cole must have never really been into me at all. His synagogue probably made him do a bunch of good deeds before his bar mitzvah, and I was just one of his charity cases. "It rocks all right," I muttered again, feeling uglier than my dress. "Everything rocks."

Max's arms stiffened around me and we were no longer moving. "You okay?"

He didn't answer me. He *couldn't* answer me. He was frozen in place like a human statue. I had turned him into a rock! He still looked like himself, but a marbleized version. My eyes darted around the room. It wasn't just Max. Everyone in the whole room was that way. I had turned everything, every*one* to be more exact, into rocks.

Totally freaky to look at—like I was in a wax museum that starred the students of Goode Middle

School. I probably would have fallen over from the sight if Max's grip wasn't holding me upright.

I needed some space to think. I tried to step back, but I had a stone prison surrounding me. Worming my way out of Max's hold was going to be a challenge. I couldn't just bust out with all my might. That would mean breaking Max's arms, and he did not deserve that. I tried shimmying my way through the small space between his hands, only I wasn't tiny enough, and pushing was definitely going to cause Max to lose a finger.

Nothing was working. Then I thought of lifting my arms and sliding out. It worked when Gabi's sister, Rori, crammed herself into her stuffed bear's miniskirt when she was five. She stood there with her arms up while Gabi and I yanked the skirt over her head. The same principal could work for my predicament, only I would slide down and out from Max's hold.

Sucking in my breath, with my hands straight up, I lowered myself. Only I couldn't get myself out. I needed more force. Someone to pull *me*. Or maybe not! The opposite could work, too. I put my hands back on Max's shoulders, and pushed as hard as I could. I got myself pretty high up off the ground. And then I slid back down again. My upper body strength wasn't exactly anything to brag about. But I didn't give up. I hoisted myself as high up as I could and managed to get one of my legs out, then the other. I was free.

"Yes!" I shouted, but quickly froze in place. Reid and Lana had just walked in. I didn't want them to see me moving around. They needed to think I was just like everyone else.

"What's going on?" Reid asked.

"I don't know, but this is creepy," Lana answered, weaving through our classmates. "Jaydin," she said, poking her friend. "Quit it. Will you say something?"

Reid tried shaking Cole. "They're like statues."

"Ohhhkayyyy," Lana shouted. "Cut it out everyone. This is not funny."

Why did they have to be late?! I didn't know how much longer I could stand there without moving. I always stunk at freeze tag. My nose would get all itchy whenever I tried to stay motionless.

Perfect. That thought was all it took for my nose to act up, and the more I thought about not scratching it, the itchier it got. It was like someone was sticking a needle in and out of my nose. The feeling was becoming unbearable, so as Lana and Reid studied their friends, I had no choice but to scratch. I tried to be as sly as I could, but the CIA wasn't going to be calling me anytime soon.

"I think she moved," Reid said, moving over to me.

Shoot! I knew he had seen me.

Lana rushed over and poked me. Hard.

"Oww," I said, not even bothering to pretend anymore. Obviously she had figured out that I wasn't a rock, and there was no way to keep them from seeing me blink.

"What is going on?" she shrieked at me. "How come you can move but no one else can?"

"Beats me," I lied, my voice wobbling. "They were all like this when I got here."

Reid grasped his neck and Lana bit her lip as she studied my face. "Then why didn't you say anything when we walked in?" she questioned me.

Because I stupidly hadn't thought to play it that way. "Um, because I was scared. I didn't know what was going on. I thought I better act like everyone else, just in case. Who knows, maybe some thief came in and told them to freeze."

"That makes no sense," she yelled. I wasn't sure if she was going to throw a hissy fit or break down in tears. But she was definitely on the brink of exploding. "A thief can't make them freeze for real."

"Well, I don't know. You explain it then," I said, trying to turn it around on her.

"Can't," Reid said. All the color had drained from his face. He pulled out his cell phone. "I'm going to call the police."

"No." I grabbed the phone from him. There were already enough people involved in my mess.

"Why not?" he demanded, looking from me to his cell.

"Because," I said, handing it back to him. "I already called. They're on their way." Giving him the sweetest smile I could muster, I added, "No need to bother them again."

Reid took Lana's hand. They grasped so hard, their knuckles were white. It was like they were holding on to each other to keep their sanity, as if letting go would suck them into this bizarre stone world.

"There's probably a completely normal explanation for everything going on," I tried to reassure them.

But there wasn't.

Not unless you considered the devil, his daughter, and out of control powers normal.

chapter
✦42✦

"I'm going to wait by the front for the cops," I told Lana and Reid. They didn't need to hear me trying to reactivate my powers. They were already spooked enough, throw in me practicing voodoo, and they probably would have tied me up and burned me at the stakes.

Bring everybody back to life, bring everybody back to life, I thought as I moved to the door. I surveyed the room. No motion—except for Lana and Reid. "Come on," I said under my breath. "Work! I need everyone to start moving again, to breathe, to become animated. Please!"

Ever so slowly, life started creeping back into the room. My classmates' expressions softened, their chests moved in and out with each breath, and they actually began to move!

"They're back," Reid yelled. But there was a problem. A major one. When he said it, his eyes bugged out. And I don't mean they got wide. They literally bugged out. Like twelve inches, maybe more.

"Yes," Lana exclaimed, and took off around the room. She made it around the whole gymnasium three times in thirty seconds, breaking every speed limit known to man.

I had made them animated all right. Like something straight out of *Looney Tunes*. I was in a room full of cartoon people.

"Angel?" Max questioned, noticing I was no longer dancing with him. He spotted me near the door and reached out. "There you are." His arm extended like someone was stretching out silly putty and pulled me back to him. "How did you get over there?"

That was his only question? Not how did he turn into Rubber Man? Or how did the Cartoon Network overtake the students of Goode Middle School? But he didn't seem to question it. No one did. They all acted like everything was normal.

And believe me, there were a lot of whacked out things going on. A few kids were climbing up the walls. Jaydin among them. Miss Simmons's feet turned into wheels and she sped out the front door, and to who knows where. This kid from homeroom flew around the room, flicking people on the head as he passed over them. When he got Courtney, she grew taller until her head almost touched the ceiling. She grabbed him and pinned him to the wall. "No one touches my hair," she screamed, her booming voice filling the whole room. "Understand?" When he nodded, she released him and shrunk back down to her normal size.

A regular-sized Courtney was bad enough; I definitely didn't need a supersized version. This needed fixing.

"Let me go, Max," I said, moving away and running over to Gabi. "Thank God, you're normal." I said when I reached her.

"Why wouldn't you be normal?" Cole asked Gabi, transforming from a balloon hanging above us back to his human form. I must say, even though it was kind of beautiful to see him float down and change into himself, I did not like seeing him as an inanimate object. He was way too cute to go around turning into random things. Not to mention that the idea of him sneaking up on me wasn't very appealing, either. What if he heard or saw something he wasn't supposed to? Although it was exciting to think that maybe he was spying on me!

"Probably because she's not normal," Gabi answered. Only she didn't speak the words. They were written out in a thought bubble over her head!

I put my finger in it and popped it. Glaring at her, I whispered, "Cut it out."

"I'm not doing it on purpose," the words formed in her next bubble. "It just happened."

"How is she *not normal*?" Cole asked, pressing Gabi for the scoop.

"She doesn't know what she's talking about," I said quickly, swatting the air above Gabi's head to make sure no more thoughts could appear there.

"That's not true." The bubble formed higher than before, way above my reach, so I couldn't get rid of it—and so that *everyone* could see. "Angel is the daughter of the devil."

"YOU'RE WHAT?!!" Courtney grew ten feet in size.

"It's a joke," I said. "Funny, right?"

The words hovering above changed to, "No joke. It's the truth." Then, "Sorry. I can't control it."

My cover was blown. My best friend had just ratted me out to the world.

"I always knew she was evil," Courtney said, pushing me backward with her huge pointer finger.

"Me? What about you. Don't you think it's weird that you suddenly have freaky growth spurts? Maybe you're the evil one," I said.

"How dare you!" Her eyes turned into slits. "I have one of the greatest gifts you can be born with."

"In what universe?"

"Okay, devil girl," she spat. "Maybe you don't know the workings of the real world because you were too busy soaking up the flames of Hades, but people in Goode are special."

I couldn't believe it. They thought all the madness around them was normal, but when it came to me and my secret—*that* they thought was messed up. Figured, my spell or whatever you wanted to call it backfired on me.

Courtney kept hold of me so I couldn't move and turned her head to face the crowd. "We better do something with her before she tries to convert us to evil."

"We should tie her up," Reid said.

"These should work," Jaydin said, crawling up the wall behind me carrying a bunch of jump ropes.

A whole slew of people moved in on me. "Yeah, don't let her get away," one yelled. "Cover her eyes so she doesn't shoot flames out," another said. "I think we should take her to Miss Simmons's class and dissect her," Lana added. "See what makes her work."

"Wait," I yelled, as two guys flew in from above to help Jaydin tie me up. "Stay away or I will make you sign over your souls." I tried to sound scary and devilish.

"Like we'd ever sign anything that you gave us," Courtney answered.

"Forget the signature, I can just say a chant and your soul is mine."

Courtney backed up a step.

"That's right," I said. "All of you move away or Lucifer's spawn will destroy you all with her evil, evil spell."

It was working. People moved back from me—that is until Gabi's thought bubble popped up in the air. "She's making all that up. She doesn't know a soul-stealing chant."

"How do you know?" Cole asked.

"She's my best friend. She tells me everything," Gabi's bubble said.

"And thought bubbles never lie," Lana nodded knowingly. "They're programmed to only display the truth."

How would she know? This was a made-up

world. "You're wrong," I cried out. No one listened. Courtney reached for a cupcake with her free hand. "We've heard enough from you devil girl." She smashed the dessert right into my mouth, then lifted me above her head.

"Let's take her to Principal Stanton, he can probe her brain."

Probe my brain?!! I didn't care what kind of crazy new world I was living in now. There was no way I was having someone mess around in my head. Let alone the principal. "Stop," I shrieked, spitting frosting everywhere. "Stop now!"

Everything went still, and there I was stuck in the air in giant Courtney's clutches.

chapter

43

There was no way down. Not without risking serious bodily harm. I was going to be stuck in Courtney's arms forever—or until someone wandered in and saw the crazy scenario and had me sent to NASA for testing.

I only had one choice. "Lou," I called quietly. Usually he appeared before I even finished saying his name, but this time there was no sign of him. "Lou," I said a little louder. Still nothing. I counted to thirty. Maybe he was busy or in the underworld and out of earshot. "Lou!" *Where was he?* I'll admit it, I was starting to panic. What if he didn't come? What would I do? "Lou, I need you. Please!"

"Ahh," he said, appearing on the ground below me. "There are your manners."

He was giving me an etiquette lesson *now*? "I really messed up," I said.

"I can see that." He folded his arms across his chest.

"Will you help? Turn everything back to before the dance started?" I needed him to do it quick. My sides were starting to hurt. Courtney's nails were stabbing me.

He shook his head. "No can do."

"What do you mean? You did it before when I caused all those problems at the musical. Just do that again."

"Sorry. I warned you. No advanced magic." He gestured to my dress, half of his mouth curling up into a smile. "And I'll hazard a guess that you didn't *buy* that outfit you have on there. You disobeyed my rules again, and now you're going to have to deal with the fallout."

"But the fallout is me perched in the sky and everyone I know frozen. You can't leave them that way. Please. Punish me, but fix them," I pleaded.

"There are consequences to your actions," he lectured.

"I know, I know, but you have to fix this."

Lou snapped his fingers, and I was instantly standing next to him. "Thank you," I said, rubbing my sides. They were probably black and blue. "Now just send us back in time."

"I already told you—no."

"But—"

He cut me off. "You need to take responsibility for what you've done. I'm not going to come in and fix all of your mess-ups, especially the ones that blatantly disobeyed my orders."

My eyes dropped to my shoes and I started chewing on my thumbnail. "So my classmates are going to be stuck like this forever? You're really not going to help them?"

"No. You are." He put his fingers under my chin and lifted my head up. "Remember your last lesson?"

"Yeah, moving the pencil backward and sending it wherever I wanted."

"Exactly, and that's what you're going to do here."

That wasn't going to work. I never mastered that one. "I can't do it," I confessed. "I don't know how."

"Sure you do." Lou took my hand. "Just like with the pencil lessons, you need to concentrate on sending it backward. Only this time, you're going to focus on rewinding time. *But*," he warned, squeezing my hand, "you never, *ever* try this without me. Otherwise you could send your friends back too far, and then there's no retrieving them."

There wasn't even a hint of playfulness in his

voice. He was serious. If I did this wrong, I could make them disappear forever. I definitely would not be trying this on my own.

"Got it?" he asked.

I nodded my head so much, I looked like one of those bobblehead dolls. "Yes."

"Okay, then," he said. "You're going to send everything back in reverse."

Focusing all of my energy, I was able to move the crowd. They slowly backed up to the wall where they had me pinned. Everyone was doing exactly what they had done before, as if I was still there (only this time it was in reverse). Gabi's thought bubbles telling everyone I couldn't take their souls showed up, then they all tried to figure out what to do with me, Jaydin and her jump ropes went back down the wall, Courtney reverted to normal size . . . It was a crazy sight. Like watching a movie on rewind, only it wasn't a movie—it was real. And it was tiring. Using this much concentrated power was draining.

I undid Gabi giving away my secret, saw Cole turn back into a balloon, people crawling down from the wall, Max's rubber arm that had extended out to me earlier shooting back to his body, Miss Simmons zooming back into the gym, and so on. By the time everyone, except for Lana and Reid, turned back to stone, I was exhausted.

"I can't do it anymore," I told Lou, and plopped myself down on the ground. "It stopped working. Please finish it for me."

"Powers are hard work. Doing something this big can zap your energy if you're not properly trained," he explained.

"Who's he?" Reid asked, moving toward us.

Uh-oh. "What's going on?" I whispered to Lou. "How come he's going forward in time?"

"Because you stopped rewinding. It set everything back in motion," Lou said. "If I were you, I'd hurry up. Otherwise your problems are going to start all over again."

Lou put out his hand and helped me up from the floor. I forced my mind to focus, and I concentrated with all my might on reversing time. I even moved my arms in a counterclockwise motion. As I did, Reid slowly reversed his steps back to his position beside Lana. I mustered up enough power for them to walk out of the gym.

I was completely zapped.

"Just a little more," Lou said, giving my shoulder a squeeze.

I closed my eyes and concentrated with all my might.

"Angel?" a voice called out. I opened my eyes and looked around. Lou was gone, but everyone else was back. To their normal, human selves, that was.

"Yes!"

"Angel?" It was Max. "Uh, how'd you get over there?"

Shoot. I was supposed to be dancing with him. Even though, I was really tired, I walked over to Max. "Sorry," I said. "Thought I dropped something."

He gave me a weird look, but he didn't question my excuse. Instead he just seemed excited to have me back. "Thanks for dancing with me."

"Sure," I answered, getting a slight case of déjà vu.

"This dance rocks," he gushed.

"Yeah, it really roc—" I stopped myself.

This time, I was keeping my mouth shut!

chapter

While I finished my dance with Max, I couldn't help but watch Cole and Jaydin. They looked so intense. I wished I had enough power and energy to send us back two and a half weeks, before I messed things up with him, or at the very least to before the dance and where I created a fashion faux pas that would make every designer on the planet cry.

But it was probably for the best. Lou was right. I needed to take responsibility for my actions. And if that meant losing Cole to mean old Jaydin or wearing a nightmare, I was going to have to live with it.

"All right, everyone," Miss Simmons called out. "It's time to name our dance king and queen."

Courtney grabbed D.L. and dragged him right to the front of the room. She was positive she was going to be crowned. I was, too.

"This was a close one," Miss Simmons said. "The king of the dance, by one vote, is . . ." She paused for dramatic effect. "D.L. Helper."

Ha! That was my vote. I didn't care that Courtney was probably beaming, because she got what she wanted and her boyfriend won. At least she wouldn't get to have her arms around *my* Cole. Well, Jaydin's Cole. But still . . .

"And the winner of queen, by a landslide . . ." Courtney reached out for the crown as Miss Simmons spoke ". . . is Angel Garrett."

"What?!" both Courtney and I shouted at the same time. People in the crowd seemed upset by it, too. "How could *she* win?" I heard one ask. "Who voted for her?" Then there were the chorus of snickers and people saying, "Look at Courtney." Boy was she fuming.

"Come on up here, Angel," Miss Simmons said, talking over the students. But I didn't budge.

Courtney stomped her foot. "This. Is. Not. Possible. No one would vote for her. She cheated."

"I supervised the voting myself," Miss Simmons said. "It was fair and square. Now come on up, Angel."

I cautiously made my way to the front, careful to avoid Courtney. She wanted to pulverize me. The whole thing was messed up. I had to agree with Courtney on this one—there had to be a mistake.

"Here you go." Miss Simmons handed me the crown.

Then everything made sense. Resting in one of the curves of the crown like he was lying on a hammock—was Lou. I turned and blocked the crown with my body so no one would be able to see.

"Congratulations," he said.

I raised an eyebrow at him.

"What?" he questioned. "You're my princess. Why shouldn't you be everyone's queen?"

So that was it. Lou rigged the vote. "I don't want to be queen," I whispered, but apparently not softly enough.

"No one else wants you to be, either," Courtney said.

I flicked Lou off the crown, turned back to Courtney and handed her the prize. "Then take it." Technically, it was hers, anyway.

She grabbed it greedily.

"Come on, girls," Miss Simmons said. She took the crown and placed it on my head. "Let's not fight. It's just a contest."

"Yeah, *my* contest," Courtney whined. "I should—"

She cut herself off when she heard someone say "pathetic." As much as she didn't want to lose, she didn't want to be made fun of for making a huge stink over it. "Whatevs," she said. "This is obviously a big practical joke. People think it's funny to see a loser win."

"Excuse me?" D.L. said.

"Well, not you," she said, trying to set things right with him. "Obviously. They think it's funny to have a loser dance with one of the popular guys."

"And speaking of dancing," Miss Simmons said, her voice trying to block out Courtney's rudeness. "It's time for our king and queen to have their spotlight number."

Uck.

Why hadn't I voted for Cole?

chapter

D.L. put his arms around me. "Now don't get too excited, Garrett. I know you've been dreaming about this since you met me." He was such a jerk.

"I'm not any happier about this than you are," I said, refusing to look directly at him. It was bad enough I was pressed up against him.

"Right," he said. "Everyone knows you're crushing on me."

"That's so not true." I had no choice but to look him straight in the eyes, otherwise he'd come up with some lame reason as to why I couldn't—like staring at him would make me confess my secret, undying love for him. As if. My heart belonged to Cole, even though he kept trying to return it. "And you better not try anything," I warned D.L. in case he got any funny ideas.

"Please, like I'd want to. Besides, I'm sure your father would kill me."

My arms dropped from his neck, and I backed up a step. "What did you say?"

"Nothing."

"What. Did. You. Say?" My hands covered my face, and I thought I was going to hyperventilate. Did D.L. see my father on the crown? Did he know my secret?

D.L. spoke under his breath. "People are staring."

"Just tell me what you said."

"I don't know. That your father would kill me," he said, his arms still around me. "Stop flipping out."

But I couldn't—this was serious. How did he know who my father was? "When did you meet my dad?" I asked, trying to get myself calm.

"Huh?"

"You heard me," I said. I began to dance again, so Miss Simmons wouldn't come up and see what was going on. I needed to know exactly what D.L. knew. "When did you meet my dad?"

"I didn't," he said, rather condescendingly.

"Then when did you *see* him?" Why did he have to be so nitpicky? I was not in the mood.

"Okay, Garrett. You're acting like a freak. I don't

know your dad, I never saw your dad, I've never heard of your dad. I was making a joke. Aren't all dads overprotective of their daughters? Jeez."

"Oh." Maybe I had overreacted just a tad. Since there wasn't really anything else I could say, I just kept dancing.

That is until someone tapped D.L. on the shoulder, and asked, "Can I cut in?"

And guess what?!

It wasn't Max. Cole Daniels wanted to dance with me!

chapter
✦ 46 ✦

D.L. seemed pretty relieved to be done with me, and I was more than happy to switch partners. Okay, that was the understatement of millennium. I was psyched and more than slightly baffled. I was about to dance with Cole! He actually asked me!

My whole body got goose bumps when I put my arms around his neck. I didn't know what to say or where to look. Did I just stare at his neck, my hands, his face? I mean, why was he there with me? It wasn't like we were exactly on speaking terms.

"Congratulations," he said.

"For what?"

"Winning queen," he said.

Duh. I should have known that. Was that why

he was there? Because I won, and he wished he had, too? That didn't seem very Cole-like, but there didn't seem to be any other explanation.

"I voted for you," he said, his eyes looking away.

What!? "You did? Why?"

Cole's cheeks turned a touch pink. "I wanted you to win."

"You're probably the only one."

"Apparently not." I forgot. As far as he knew, a ton of people voted for me.

We didn't say anything for a minute, we just danced. But I couldn't really enjoy it. There was still something pressing on my mind. "What about Jaydin? She's going to be angry that you're dancing with me. I'm not exactly her favorite person."

He shrugged his shoulders.

I waited for him to explain.

"We broke up," he said.

Was I his consolation prize because his girlfriend dumped him? Would he go running back to her if she changed her mind? "Oh." Cole didn't go into detail about what happened, but I needed to know. "Why?"

"I didn't like the way she talked to Max . . . or about you." He looked right at me and gave me one of his amazing lopsided grins. "But I thought it was pretty cool the way you came to Max's defense."

Suddenly everything made sense. Cole and Jaydin didn't look super intense when they were dancing because they were expressing their love for each other. It was because they were breaking up.

I smiled back at him. "I'm really sorry for the way I've been acting."

"It was weird. One minute you were carving into my tree, the next you wouldn't even speak to me."

This time I knew I was the one with the pink cheeks. He had to go and mention the tree? I couldn't look at him. "I got embarrassed after you saw the initials. I realized it may have been too much too soon."

"Maybe a little," he said. "But it was kinda cute."

All that worrying and he thought it was kinda cute!

"And then there was everything going on with my dad, it made me kind of bonkers," I confessed.

"You could have told me about him," he said. "I would have understood."

That's what he thought. "I know. It's just complicated." I glanced down at my feet and then back up at him. "You forgive me?"

He nodded and our eyes locked. My pulse moved to turbo speed and fireworks started exploding in my stomach. Only this time I was able to keep them there as Cole moved in close and finally kissed me.

Shani Petroff is a writer living in New York City.
Bedeviled: The Good, the Bad, and the Ugly Dress
is the second book in the Bedeviled series. She also
writes for news programs and several other venues.
When she's not locked in her apartment typing away,
she spends a whole lot of time on books, boys, TV,
daydreaming, and shopping online. She'd love for you
to come visit her at www.shanipetroff.com.

bedeviled

CAREFUL WHAT YOU WISH FOR

Will Angel's powers ever stop
getting her into trouble?

 Find out in the next
installment of Bedeviled:
Careful What You Wish For

bedeviled

Do you have special powers like Angel?
Take this quiz to expose the strength of your hidden talents.

1) You spot your crush across the crowded cafeteria and . . .

A) you attempt to stride confidently to your table, but
then spill your lunch tray all over the floor.

B) you give him a covert wink and, like a magnet, he starts heading your way.

C) you smile and, miraculously, he looks your way and smiles back—but then
the class flirt whisks him away before anything else happens.

2) During an English exam, you think you are hearing voices. These voices . . .

A) recite the notes you studied last night.

B) sing the lyrics to your favorite song in *High School Musical*.

C) give you all the right answers, despite your lack of studying.

3) You're at the hottest concert of the year and your dad shows up. You . . .

A) silently wish you were invisible and suddenly come to realize no one can see
you, including the parental unit.

B) end up standing next to him all night, wishing the earth would swallow you

C) try to hide from him all night and hope that you aren't grounded in the morni

4) You're home daydreaming about your crush and the phone rings. It's . . .

A) your crush calling to ask you out.

B) your mother, who is running late and wants you to start
dinner.

C) your best friend, to say she overheard your crush
talking about you at the mall.

**5) You're at the dance ALONE, feeling sorry for yourself
as usual, when you spot your crush and worst enemy slow
dancing together. You make a silent wish for him to stop
everything and ask you to dance. What happens next?**

A) Nothing. He keeps dancing with the enemy and you drown
your sorrows by the punch bowl.

B) You accidentally look over at the school geek and he thinks
you're in love with him. You can't shake him all night.

C) Your crush immediately looks over, stops dancing with the
enemy, and heads your way, asking, "Ummm hey, do you want
to dance?"

To reveal your special powers, write down your answers and
then visit penguin.com/bedeviled to reveal how powerful
you really are!